Secret Violent Desires

First Edition

Published by The Nazca Plains Corporation
Las Vegas, Nevada
2007

ISBN: 978-1-934625-29-3

Published by

The Nazca Plains Corporation ®
4640 Paradise Rd, Suite 141
Las Vegas NV 89109-8000

PUBLISHER'S NOTE
Secret Violent Desires is a work of fiction created wholly by *Dan Erickson's* imagination. All characters are fictional and any resemblance to any persons living or deceased is purely by accident. No portion of this book reflects any real person or events.

Cover, Fleshblack
Art Director, Blake Stephens

DEDICATION

"He that wrestles with us strengthens our nerves, and sharpens our skill. Our Antagonist is our helper."

Edmond Burke

1729 - 1727

Secret Violent Desires

First Edition

Dan Erickson

CONTENTS

LOOKING FOR CRAIG

Gary looked at the picture on the screen. "Shit, this guy is huge," he said to himself under his breath. Gary was right. The guy's name was Craig Barret and he had a huge frame, square shoulders, a well-developed broad chest that rippled down to a rugged set of abs. In the picture he stood on a rural set of train tracks, not really flexing, casually regarding the camera. His ears stuck out like a pair of radar dishes. As weird as that sounded, Gary always found that to be dangerously attractive.

Craig's web profile bragged about his wrestling and football ability. But the hook in Gary's mind, "I love to wrap men in my muscular arms and crush them!!" To make it all beautiful, Craig was 19 years old, just two years younger than he was.

Craig was what Gary had dreamed of for years; a big man that loves to wrestle and advertises. No mysteries, come here and get wrapped in solid muscle for the crush of your life, but Gary also knew about the stories people get to tell about themselves when it comes to wrestling. This could all be a manufactured ID. He could be a little wiry-haired poodle in New Jersey named Himey. Craig said he was in Idaho.

He punched the name "Craig Barret" into the internet white

pages. Sure enough, Craig Barret, Emmett, Idaho. He exists. And there he was, chatting away with thirty other guys in the "TeenMusclePower" chat room.

Gary knew he was going on an insane journey the minute he clicked on Craig's name to chat with him. What if he likes me? Gary decided he would try to become friends. But what if he liked that? Well, then he'd find out if they could meet. But what if he says yes? Well, he'd buy a plane ticket and fly to Idaho, if necessary.

"Hello little man," Craig's IM said.

Gary tried not to be nervous. Craig warned that the locals liked to talk a lot and promised their meeting might be short with precautions to ensure privacy. Gary wondered if that was an attempt to say that he really didn't want him to come. *Bad time to think of it*, Gary said to himself. The plane trip to Boise was strangely expensive. He had tickets all across the country cost less. There was turbulence for the landing and he knew he was sweating. "I hope I look okay," he said under his breath.

"You look fine," muttered the woman sitting next to him in First Class. He was sitting in First Class because there were no other seats available on the limited flights. She had a heavy New York accent.

"You meeting your sweetie?" She looked like the scary aunt that everyone has. She was probably the one that all the kids run from on Thanksgiving because she wore frightening makeup, her breath smelled like garlic, and she pinched their cheeks too much.

"Um, no...Really I'm going for a job interview." Gary said.

"Oh, you can't fool Mrs. Genie," the woman said with the flip of her hand. "I yenta for so many guys back home. Get them put together with the right sweetie. You look just like the ones that meet the right girl - JUST like them! Just look at you. You're young and muscled up real nice. Who wouldn't like you? You'll be fine."

He was reassured a small bit by her appraisal. He really he thought he was too short for Craig being only 5'8'. He had a Spanish mother and an Italian father. They gave him dark brown eyes, a thick furrowed brow, and model handsome square jawed features. He'd lifted since he was fifteen and wrestled since he was sixteen. He wore a tight olive silk shirt over khaki pants. The shirt showed off his muscled torso very well, even hinting at his tight six-pack. But he didn't take into account the way sweat showed through these things when he was nervous.

"So what's her name? Tell Mrs. Genie," she was smiling bigger than a tire iron.

"Really, it's not what you think..."

"Oh Romeo, what's her name, you HAVE to tell Mrs. Genie."

The whole plane lurched in the turbulent winds over Boise. Gary took a deep breath. "His name is Craig and he's about 6 foot 4 inches tall, has huge muscles, and wants to wrestle me before we have an evening of Italian food and passionate animalistic sex. At which point, I think we'll probably decide what happens when he gets out of the Marines."

The woman blanched. She blinked twice. "Craig." She said just to see how it sounded. "That's a man."

"Oh yes, he is that," Gary said.

"And you looked like such a nice boy," she was crestfallen. "You know dear, I think Mrs. Genie is out of her league on this one."

"I thought you might say that," Gary said smiling. "Actually I thought you'd run from me screaming. You're a tough old bird."

She sparkled and took the comment as a compliment. "Well, thank you. I am, and don't forget it! Besides, we have plenty in common. I go to mush over tall muscular men, too."

"I don't look mushy, do I?"

"NO! you're strong, sturdy...he likes you right?"

"Oh yeah," Gary said. And Craig sure did. That first night Gary received four e-mails and a shipment of flowers the next day. They were daisies. He talked on line for three hours the next night and then on the phone for four more. His voice was deep and curious. He asked questions all the time.

"He likes you, you'll be fine." With that comment, she retreated into her magazine and let Gary go back into his rumination.

He thought about Craig and what he should say to him when they meet. Everything that he rehearsed came out like a sleazy pick-up line from a porn movie. Maybe that's all he had at his disposal, sleazy pick-up lines. *What am I doing here?*

He realized he didn't think much about what he wanted from Craig. He imagined asking a waiter to bring Craig and tell him what he really wanted.

"Yes, I would like a tall white guy, heavy on muscle, preferably some variation of blond, good skill at wrestling, passionate, tough, oh yeah, and willing to wrap his arms around me and squeeze me tight, and a ten-inch cock wouldn't be too much."

"Will you be having him here, or is he to go?"

"Here."

He pictured meeting Craig in the airport, his huge shoulders taking up the space of a couple normal people. He pictured coming off the plane and seeing him there and walking toward him. They both smile. Craig reaches his hand out for a handshake. Gary runs at him and tackles him, hitting him squarely in the chest with his right shoulder.

Caught off guard, but trained in reflex, Craig instinctively wrapped an arm around Gary's head on their way to the floor and rolls Gary toward the floor. Not really caring how he landed, Gary took the brunt of the fall catching most of Craig's weight as they hit the floor. They hit with a grunt.

Now on his back with Craig on top of him, Gary grabbed Craig's wrist and pulled in between his legs. As he hoped, Craig was off balance enough. He just pulled to free his arm. Gary's short but thick legs flashed up wrapping behind Craig's head. He quickly cinched a figure four catching Craig's neck and right arm and shoulder. Craig fell onto his back as Gary tightened up this suffocating figure-four chokehold. Gary kept this in tight control holding onto Craig's wrist.

Gary looked into Craig's deep blue eyes as he squeezed with all of his strength. In a display of raw power, Craig flexed his chest and shoulders, prying his throat out of the constricting embrace. He shook his wrist free and with his elbow, pressed into Gary's gut until his scissors hold popped open.

Gary scrambled to get free while Craig got his balance back. That was not happening. It took no time for Craig to slip his huge arm around Gary's midsection. He brought his other arm around and Gary felt the closing embrace he wanted for so long. Those heavy muscled arms slipped around him in a warm flow. "I got you now, little man," Craig said as he clamped his pythons tight behind Gary's back. He could smell Craig. It was like warm cedar. Gary's cock hardened and pressed into the beautiful abdominal wall of Craig. The squeeze began and Gary was in heaven. It was like a buzz of tiny voices cheered around him while he and Craig started humping each other with a furious abandon.

Then it all shattered.

"SECURE THE CABIN FOR LANDING," The Captain announced, jarring Gary out of his daydreams. There was a bustle of activity where their stewardess collected glasses, napkins, and peanut wrappers. Gary tried to hide his stiff cock straining his pants after his vivid nap. He really didn't want to fasten his seat belt.

The landing took forever, or so it seemed. He walked down the bridge to the terminal and saw a crowd of people waiting for the people getting off the plane. Her family greeted the woman he sat next to. They all screeched and made similar noises. The children present were silent. True to Gary's prediction, she pinched each one of them on the cheek and they winced at the unwanted attention. He was grateful he wasn't attending this sort of family reunion. He looked around and saw no one that looked like Craig's profile picture. He was getting nervous. Maybe this is a big mistake. Then he saw him. It was a huge guy standing with a brown cardboard sign that said, "Gary."

The crowd dwindled and thinned. He began to wonder if he had been taken. Surely this couldn't be Craig. He was big. His chest pressed the fishing vest he wore into a hard broad shape. The small beer gut was a surprise. So was the mustache. His hair was blond, but not the golden color he expected. It looked more like cement than blond. The man had thick defined legs that showed through his old blue denim. Check that, they were truly huge. Thighs like that could be very powerful. It was just enough to keep Gary interested. His old wranglers showed off his ass nicely as well.

He told himself that he really felt attraction to the young man Craig, not necessarily his appearance. But then he was sure it was just appearance. He remembered himself buying the ticket online with a stiff woodie. He began to curse himself for letting his little head think for him. He decided to get this going.

He walked up to the man with the sign. "You're Craig?"

"Yup," the guy said with a smile. One of his front teeth was missing. Gary was sure he blinked in disbelief even when he tried to control his body. "Um..." Gary couldn't even form words. He didn't want to seem like he was just in love with appearances. But he decided to be honest. This time he was.

"You don't look like your profile picture."

"You don't either," Craig said. "You look even better."

"You didn't tell the truth," Gary said. "I really think this isn't going to work."

"Did you come here to wrestle me or are we going to pick out silverware?" He asked Gary. "Okay, let's get to your hotel and get to know each other. If you're not happy still, I'll put you on the next plane tomorrow."

"You can't afford that."

"I got some money," the man said. "Besides, what can happen in a hotel? I don't even have to come to your room."

Gary really felt like he was being a dick when he looked into his eyes. The look betrayed the nineteen year old man, hopeful and confused. "Okay, let's have dinner. I'm really hungry."

"So am I," said Craig. With that, he picked up Gary's gym bag and they went to the parking lot.

Craig drove an old Ford Ranger, white with spots of rust betraying its age. There was a plow rack on the front. The bed of the truck was full of wrappers for roof shingles. The inside was not much better. It was full of beer cans and McDonald's bags and wrappers. Gary really felt like getting rest. It was going to be a long night. Gary's bag was dropped into the bed of the truck. The truck was unlocked and he got in. He closed the door and fumbled for a seat belt.

Gary never saw the man pull the spray container from his vest pocket. Gary sat in his seat and caught a fiery spray in his face and instantly couldn't see. A huge fist hit him in the face. And again. He lost consciousness as hit his head on the dashboard.

When he awoke, Gary's body was in a riot of pain. His face hurt. He expected that. He tried to move and found that his arms were bound behind him, actually behind the seat. He was really glad he kept up on his shoulder stretches. He was sure he'd dislocate his shoulder if he tried to pull on his bonds. He felt it with his fingers. They were numb.

The whole cab of the truck lurched as they hit a bump. He opened his eyes. It was near dark and they just turned to a mountainous road. It was rough and painful. His captor turned his attention from driving to him.

"Hey, you're awake." He smiled his broken smile. "You're quite a stud. you must spend time in those city gyms, huh?" He rubbed his hand over Gary's six-pack abs. Gary's saw his shirt was pulled out of his pants and his fly was open. *This fucker must've had fun with me while I was out.* "You feel real nice."

"You're not Craig," Gary concluded out loud.

"Ooooo, you're smart too," he said mockingly. "Well sort of smart. Still not smart enough to avoid getting into someone's truck when you don't know him. I bet you even take candy from strangers. Well, we'll find out."

Gary didn't like the sound of that. The truck hit another hard bump. They were driving into a glade of trees far from most roads. Another bump. His right shoulder wrenched hard and he closed his eyes in pain. "This hurts, man. Do you have to tie me up so tight? I can't feel my hands."

"Aaaawww, you're complaining. I can stop that," he stopped the truck and pulled a roll of duct tape out of the cargo pocket in the driver's door. "MacGyver would be proud." He pulled off a length of tape and slapped it over Gary's mouth. Gary tried to bite him but missed. The man slapped him in the head. "Bad dog! You will be punished for that."

There was a thunderous eruption under the truck. The truck stopped suddenly. The man had a fearful look on his face. "You wait here," he said. Then he chuckled at the comment. "Not like you have any choice." The man got out of the truck and pulled a pair of handcuffs and a nightstick from the back seat. He left the door open and looked under the truck.

Then Gary heard another voice. "Four flat tires. Imagine that. What are the odds?" A tall man with a flashlight emerged from the woods in front of the truck. The unmistakable features of the blond hair and blue eyes were visible. It was the real Craig.

He looked in the windshield at Gary, "Hey Little Man. You okay?"

Gary couldn't respond. He was so thrilled to see Craig that he wanted to scream.

Craig waited to hear a response and didn't get one. "you are way out of line, Buford," the real Craig said. "I don't know how you knew about him, but you're gonna pay for this one."

"You're sister has a big mouth, Craig," Buford gloated. "She not only talks a lot, her mouth's big enough to take my cock."

"I knew that. Not surprising," He closed distance with Buford. "Your brother has a big mouth, too. And a big dick now that you mention it."

"You touched my brother?" Buford said in a trembling rage.

"No. I fucked your brother. He begged me."

Buford rushed Craig with that. He flailed with the nightstick in rage. Craig ducked the overhead swing easily and moved in, landing a fist in Buford's beer gut with a thump. Gary saw Buford fumbling in his vest pocket. Gary knew this was trouble and didn't feel like waiting quietly while Craig was maced and beaten. Gary pulled on his bonds and knew this was hopeless. He closed his eyes thinking and came up with a plan.

He planted his feet on the dashboard and arched backward. The chair was not going to break. *Okay. Something else.* He kicked his feet to the dashboard and walked the ceiling of the cab pulling him over the seat. He felt blessed for being short and flexible. A taller man could not do this. He landed in the trash heap in the back and heard Craig scream in pain. He took three deep breaths through his nose to keep himself from panicking. He hoped he could free himself before it was too late.

He wriggled his bound hands under his butt in front of him. He felt nothing in his hands at the moment and knew that was a small blessing. He tumbled between the bucket seats of the truck and out the driver's door. He crawled slowly around the corner of the truck to look at where they stood.

Craig was rolling on the ground in pain. Buford was handcuffing Craig's right wrist to the plow rack at the front of the truck. He fumbled for the night stick in the leaves on the ground. With his back turned to Gary, Buford's legs flexed. They were huge. *Must be the only asset on this ugly prick.*

When he got the stick in his hands, he stood over Craig. It was clear Craig was not able to see him yet, still trying to wipe the spray from his eyes. Using the stick like a spear, he drove it into Craig's gut hard. Craig wolfed a groan as his abs were punished. "NEVER" he speared his gut again. "CALL" spear! "ME" Spear! "BUFORD!" He punctuated his order with a heavy boot to Craig's face. "My name is Ford!"

Craig coughed hard trying to get his breath back. He flexed his stomach showing muscle through his shirt. Gary marveled at the development on this guy. Buford kicked him good in the face. Blood poured freely from Craig's nose. *That had to hurt.* In a weird moment, Gary felt a wave of relief that Craig really hadn't staged this whole thing.

With one hand still free, Craig managed to grab Buford's foot blocking the next kick. With a turn of his wrist, plopped the big assailant on his butt. *He just turned that huge leg...* Gary was in awe of Craig's strength.

Using the stick like a spear, he struck Craig in the gut again. He smacked Craig in the left elbow turning his free arm useless. He hammered Craig's triceps half a dozen times quickly, still on his butt next to the poor stud. "I like this part. I hear you do too," he said as he slipped his legs around Craig. Trying to fend off his attacker, Craig pushed with his left arm. Buford pushed his defense away and turned his huge arm behind his back in a hammerlock.

He crossed his ankles around Craig's waist. "Let's see if you can breathe through this." He straightened his legs and clamped his body scissors on him tightly. Craig wailed in pain. "Ugggggh! you fucker."

"Oh, that's next," said Buford. "I'll fuck your unconscious body. Then I'll fuck your little friend." He made his meaning clear by squeezing Craig even harder. Craig's face reddened as his punished midsection was squeezed without mercy. A long crying groan was wrenched from his throat as he tried to fight off the squeeze. He struggled violently, trying to drag them both closer to the truck so he could use his trapped powerful right arm. Buford's thick quads were cutting a dent in Craig's midsection, deeply crushing the young muscle stud.

Gary had seen enough. He still couldn't get his hands free but he had to get in there. If Craig were punished much more, he wouldn't be useful in this fight any more. Gary couldn't stop his heart from racing but he was decided. He popped up to his feet and rushed the pair. He leapt at Buford with both feet connecting with Buford's head. He lurched back but didn't break his crushing body lock on Craig. Straddling his waist with his back to Craig, Gary tried pummeling Buford with two-fisted blows.

Letting go of the hammerlock, Buford's strong hands blocked Gary's further attacks. He slipped his arms around Gary and clasped a bearhug around his back. Gary felt like a fool, as he was included in the crushing embrace. Planting his chin on Gary's sternum, Buford tightened his muscular biceps around him. At the same time he wrenched his thighs tighter around Craig's bruised abs. Both Craig and Gary felt their ribs bend under crushing power of the double hold.

Craig had a free hand but couldn't get an effective attack on Buford without hitting Gary. He pushed at the crossed ankles and tried to get free. With a pumping squeezing motion, Buford pulsed the constriction around Craig's straining middle. Craig groaned in pain.

Giving up on Buford's legs, Craig reached up to try the handcuffs. Gary tried to head butt Buford in the face and felt the same crushing pulse as Buford rearranged his ribs with more muscular power. He turned to see what Craig was doing and barely saw his success. Craig couldn't break the hold or the cuffs, but Buford's rusted truck was not a problem. With a double handed twist, he popped the rusted weld in the plow rack and the handcuffs came free.

Unbound and pissed, Craig pushed with his powerful legs and lifted all three men up onto Buford's back. Taking his chances, Buford threw Gary aside with a heave and turned to face Craig alone. Face to face, still trapped between Buford's legs, Craig struggled to land a punch or elbow.

Gary caught his breath and tried to regain his feet. He was going to kick that bastard in the head until he was prettier. He saw Craig, red faced as Buford turned on the hardest crushing constriction he could summon. Fumbling through the leaves, Craig came up with the nightstick.

Buford's head swiveled to the left as Craig's powerful arms drove the stick into his face. Not wanting to be left out, Gary landed a kick to Buford's head. The pythonic embrace around Craig's waist slackened and Buford's eyes rolled back into his head. Gary kicked him again. He tried to land another kick and was blocked by Craig.

"Stop, he's out."

"No fucking way!!" Gary howled struggling to get past Craig and his bonds. "That bastard tried to rape me! He kidnapped me!"

Craig wrapped his arms around Gary's head and held him to his chest. "Shhhhh, quiet now."

"You be quiet! I'm killing him!"

Strong hands wrapped around Gary's face and hauled him up to look into Craig's eyes. "You listen. We can't do it this way."

"Why not?!" Gary asked as tears of anger leaked from his face. Gary closed his eyes, embarrassed at his clash of emotions.

"If we hurt him any more, his friends will harass my family for years. There will be no end to this. Right now, it's his embarrassing secret and my trump card," Craig explained.

"I don't care. I want him dead!" Gary shouted.

Gary felt a stab of fire in his left shoulder. There was a swirl of color and nausea as he fell to the ground. He heard the sound of struggle and came around in time to see Craig catch a taser point in the chest. He clutched it and fought hard against the flowing charge robbing his muscular body of control. A second point hit him on the other side of his chest just as he pulled the first out. His head jerked back and he landed on the ground with his eyes pinned open.

When the juice stopped, his eyes closed. He lay still. Gary knew they were both in serious trouble. He closed his eyes and played dead. Maybe they were going to leave him alone. Gary kept his eyes closed and kept his body limp. He swore he heard people in the woods talking. Well, it was more like whispers. He was dragged from the woods into the truck again and the heavy load dumped in the bed of the truck he presumed was Craig. Without a word, a driver got in the car and gunned the engine.

He felt the scatter of garbage in the cab of the truck – feeling around for a weapon of some sort. His hands fell on something that felt like pliers. It took him a few minutes to slowly rotate the object in his hand. He discovered they were wire cutters. *Not a killing weapon, that's for sure,* he said to himself. He kept them in his hand anyway, hoping to drop them in exchange for something else more useful.

It was not a long drive. They stopped after only a few minutes of driving. While he was feeling like he was mostly recovered from the shock, he made himself stay limp. The door of the truck popped open without the driver opening his door. He almost opened his eyes in surprise, but stayed calm.

Heavy hands grabbed his body and hefted him over a muscular shoulder. His carrier wore a thin T-shirt. Gary could feel the muscle on this guy through the shirt.

"You better explain to me why my toys are already beat up," said the carrier in a rumbling low voice. I paid you guys to bring the little guy here and Craig would follow. Now he's all beat up."

"What's the difference?" Gary heard Buford wise off. Gary was dumped on the ground in the wet grass.

"I'll tell you the difference!" There was a sinister meanness in that voice. "I want my toys to have eyes I can look into and see the fear on their faces as I have my fun! I think you want to stand in for them tonight, don't you?" There was the unmistakable sound of a fist hitting a face.

Buford howled like a dog, injured. He was smacked four more times and he just stopped trying to make words and just whimpered. "Karl, I wanted to but Roger tasered them when they were trying to beat me up and I..."

"Will you LOOK at him!" shouted Karl, the mean one. "He's already unconscious! Buford, get in your truck and go home. I don't want to see you for a week!" The car door slammed and there was the sound of Buford peeling away.

There was silence in the wake of Buford's exit.

Whispers from the grass filled the air, just for a moment. Gary strained his ears to hear – it wasn't insects. It was more like a restless audience.

Another set of footsteps slowly walk toward Gary on the wet grass. The whispering was drowned out by voice. "Karl, you still up for playin?"

"Roger, shut up," Karl said, much calmer. "The little fairy is out cold. He might even be dead. I don't care. He's an outsider. But Craig, shit, man! I had plans for him!" He paced while Roger lit a cheap smelling cigar. "I'm horny as all hell, and I have to wait for the stud to wake up."

"You're one sick fucker," Roger said walking away.

"I love you too," Karl said. "Remind me to kill Buford after this."

"Don't worry, Buford will remind you," Roger said. "He's that kinda stupid."

Gary felt himself being dragged across the grass. A metal sliding shed door opened and the sound of a table unfolding played out of the soundless interior. Gary was hoisted in the air and strapped to the table. It was a bad job as he had hoped. He could feel all kinds of wiggle room in his bonds. He could be out in a couple of minutes.

The shed was left open as the footsteps receded into the distance. Gary risked a look around. The shed was much larger than he expected. This thing must be30 feet per side, ten feet high. There was a single bulb hanging in the center of the shed casting harsh light with sharp shadows. Gary could hear them coming back. Keeping his eyes half open, he tested the strap holding him to the table. It was loosely slung over his chest and arms. All he really had to do was raise his arms over his head and he'd be able to push out of it, unless there were surprises in there he couldn't see.

It took both men to carry Craig. He was flopped on a table next to Gary. Looking around slowly through half open eyes, Gary could see there were electric appliances attached to dildoes, a few leather straps,a flogger out of braided black leather, a riding crop and the nightstick. And silicon sex lube on the shelf over Craig's table. They planned on fucking him, that's for sure.

Craig was laid on the table and secured in place with white plastic zip ties, thin strips of packing plastic, but very hard to break. These were a half-inch wide. Gary was sure he couldn't break them if he were held with those, but he wasn't sure about Craig. Roger drank deeply from a beer bottle as Karl worked. Roger was not as muscular as Karl, but if Roger made as much effort in the gym as Karl seemed to, he'd be bigger. His shoulders were wide like Karl's, but his beergut was just beginning to grow.

Karl stood under the light. He had huge pecs that cast round shadows over his ribbed abs. His sharp nipples pointed down. He slowly stripped his T-shirt off. Karl took the beer out of Roger's hand and dumped it on Craig's head.

He awoke sputtering, trying to get up. Gary could tell when he really knew where he was. He stopped struggling. "Hey Karl, you sick fucker. I'm not surprised. You'd better kill me."

Karl reached up to the shelf and grabbed an appliance that looked like a clothing iron. It had a coil over a handle. Karl tore a hole in Craig's T-shirt, laid the flat of the iron to Craig's pec, and pressed the red button. The light dimmed as a charge of sparking voltage pumped through Craig's chest, sizzling on his skin.

Screaming in pain, flexing every muscle in his huge chest, arching off the table, Craig writhed as he endured his punishment. The juice stopped and Karl replaced the iron. Panting a scream with each breath, Craig slowly recovered. He pulled as hard as he could on his restraints, hoping they would pop open. Roger ran his hands across Craig's chest and down his abs unconcerned about Craig's attempts to escape. He felt each of Craig's thighs and made it clear he enjoyed the struggles and muscles of this captive super stud.

Roger pulled a big hunting knife from his back pocket and cut Craig's shirt off his chest. Craig went still. From neckline to navel he let the knife slowly rip the shirt exposing his muscular torso. He rubbed his hands on bare skin. "I like this one, Karl."

"I'm going to torture you, as I promised," Karl said. "I was hoping to make your little fairy guest watch, but he's out cold."

"I'm gonna get you, bastard..." Craig stopped talking as he saw Karl reach for the iron. Seeing he stopped, Karl replaced the iron.

"See Roger, he can be taught," Karl said.

Gary heard a truck pulling up to the shed. Both men straightened up and looked like they had just been caught. "Mother," hissed Roger.

"Shut up, dumbass!" Karl hissed back. He pulled out a roll of duct tape and sealed Craig's mouth.

"What are you boys doing in there so late?" An old woman's voice asked. It was like listening to Norman Bates answer his mother as these bumbling guys ran outside to rattle on to their mother how they're fixing a broken lawn mower because they really need it tomorrow.

Gary wasted no more time. He slipped himself out of the strap restraint and jumped over to his buddy. Craig's eyes snapped open when he saw Gary clipping the restraints –hand, ankle, ankle, hand – and was done in a flash. He quickly laid back on his table. As an afterthought, he jumped up and unplugged the iron, smiling devilishly at Craig. He kissed the young stud on the forehead.

"You ok?" Gary whispered. Craig nodded as a tear leaked out of his eye. "Just relax and fuck these bastards up," Gary said. He flashed back onto his table to resume his coma.

"Well, you boys don't stay out here too late," Mother's voice rasped. "I want you ready for work tomorrow."

"Yes, mother," the boys intoned. Gary was ready with his clippers to gouge any one of them that noticed he was unrestrained. They paid him no mind. Craig lay still on the table as they came back. "Now where were we?" Karl said.

"Can I hear him scream again, Karl?" Roger asked quietly. "It'll get my wood back."

Karl smiled big, "Sure." He reached for the iron and set it on Craig's abdomen. "You like the sound of a guy getting his guts cooked?"

"I don't know Karl, let's see," Roger said. Karl hit the red button.

Nothing happened. He hit it again with a puzzled look on his face. His puzzled expression turned to fear when he saw Craig begin to move. The expression didn't live long as Craig's fist smashed Karl's nose flattening it. Roger never even registered shock or fear. He was in disbelief as Craig's big size 14 foot connected with his jaw.

Gary scrambled for the door with Karl and Roger fleeing behind him. Craig flew and tackled all three men.

Gary rolled and skidded in the wet grass. He sat up to see Craig astride Roger, landing heavy punches to his face again and again. Karl rolled and landed on his feet apparently. Pulling a length of wire from his pocket, he slipped behind Craig in an attempt to garrote him.

The wire coiled around Craig's throat pulling his head back, nearly lifting him off Roger. Karl's brother crab-walked back to get away from Craig. He bawled and held his face. Karl leaned forward to bear as much force on the wire around Craig's neck as he could. Craig's neck muscles stood out like steel as the wire pressed in on his throat.

Karl fell on his butt and pulled Craig between his legs. Fighting the cord around his neck with his hands, Craig was unable to stop those huge legs wrapping around him. Karl crossed his ankles and squeezed. A strangled groan leaked from Craig's throat as he held tough to take the pressure closing around him. Seeing that Karl had him in hand, Roger paid no attention to Craig and held his face. "By ndoze! you boke by doze! Blood leaked through Roger's hands and dripped down his elbows.

Craig powered up to his knees, lifting Karl off the ground. Karl squeezed Craig without mercy, holding on to him with his crushing body scissors.

First with one foot and then the other, Craig stood. Roger saw this and rushed to tackle him. Craig's booted foot plowed into Roger's face. Roger went down and Craig followed. He fell forward onto his knees, planting his face on the ground. With inexorable momentum, Karl pitched over Craig's head. Gary gasped. This would either free him, pulling the wire out of Karl's hands, or it would kill him, ripping Craig's head off.

Karl rolled forward and landed on his face-smashed brother. A boot to Karl's head and a stomp to Roger's guts, both brothers were rolling in pain. Karl was on all fours, shaking his head. Craig straddled Karl's head and fell to his side, trapping Karl in a painful head scissors. Through his blue jeans, Gary saw Craig's striated muscles leap hard and press Karl's head in a viselike grip. Roger, still rolling in pain, came too close. Craig wrapped his arms around Roger's gut from behind.

The double python squeeze crushed into the sick pair of brothers. Karl's muffled scream echoed out from between Craig's legs. Roger barely let out a groan as those 20" biceps closed on his waist, cutting off his ability to inhale.

Feeling like Craig had the affair in hand, Gary watched as Karl's struggles became weaker. Roger stopped moving long before Karl, but even the more muscular of the two was eventually squeezed into limp submission.

Craig let them go and stood before Gary. A stiff erection could be seen in his pants. Gary saw his handsome fighter man and his pants suddenly fit badly. Gary looked around and could see from the dim houselights that they were in a field near a large wooded area.

Craig walked toward him and took Gary by the hand. "Come

on," he said quietly. He ran into the woods, effortlessly finding a path that cut through the dense scrub on the fringe of the trees. Gary followed at the same pace.

Once in the denser part of the forest, Gary found himself blind. Huge arms slipped around him from behind. He could feel the intense heat flowing off of Craig's muscular body. His skin was like marble. Craig surrounded Gary in a squeeze and nuzzled at the nape of his neck, just behind the ear.

"I want you. Strip!" Craig ordered. Gary found himself completely naked and in Craig's embrace in a matter of seconds. He felt Craig's huge cock press into his stomach. He kissed Gary deeply holding his buddy in an engulfing embrace. Gary felt behind his balls, gently caressing him. His cock leaked in anticipation. They slipped to the ground, uncaring about the sticks and dirt. "I want to fuck you."

"You don't have any lube, you'll kill me with that thing," Gary said. From his back pocket, Craig pulled out the tube of lube that was on Karl's utility shelf.

"I'm prepared," Craig said. Gary knew he was smiling wickedly. "Git it up to me."

Gary lifted his legs and felt Craig enter him. It was burningly painful at first. A hot pleasure flowed over his body and he clenched his ass in rhythm, massaging his lover's pounding cock. Craig moaned in delirious pleasure. Craig humped Gary like a wild animal. Gary wrapped his arms around Craig's shoulders, clutching that fabulous muscular body while he was pistoned into the ground.

Craig pumped surging spurts of cum into Gary's ass, lifting Gary clean off the ground, rearing up on his knees. Gary heard whispers in the woods, like words coming from the wind. Craig roared as he came more and hammered Gary bodily onto his cock.

Whispers.

Gary was hard as a rock and came when Craig wrapped his arms around him. He came on Craig's chest gluing them together as they lay on the ground in their hot afterglow.

Whispers of a hundred small voices.

Craig lifted Gary from the ground and brushed dirt off his naked body. The whispers had stopped and Gary followed Craig through the woods until they emerged in a small clearing. There was a log cabin, a summer lodge for sure. Craig brazenly walked into the front door.

There was a huge bed in this cabin and nothing more. With a romantic flourish, Craig lifted Gary off his feet and dropped him on the bed. "Sleep!" he said, a hand waving gently over his face.

As ordered, Gary dropped into a deep sleep, instantly. Magically.

Craig washed his face and toweled his body off. He walked out to the porch and stood looking into the deep darkness of the woods. "Well?" he said aloud.

Like wind singing through the branches, a voice sounded as if a hundred thin voices sang in unison, "You were very entertaining. Your offering of blood and seed has been well received. Your wish is granted, human."

"So you'll protect my family when I'm gone?"

"As long as you wish it," said the whispers. Craig smiled. He knew he should probably thank Gary for his part in this act, but he's a city kid and wouldn't understand. Spirits of the woods are fickle. They could turn on Ma or Dad while he was away with the Marines at war. He wanted to make sure they were going to be friendly before he was too old to hear them any more.

He turned and snuggled into bed with Gary. Wrapped in Craig, Gary slept. Rapt with Craig, the land rejoiced in nightsong.

PLEASE

Time had abandoned me. I was stranded outside the locker rooms waiting. I had already counted all the change in my pocket. I had done 250 push-ups. I had even mentally balanced the checkbook my father insisted I have. I counted 10,001 gum chews as I chewed my gum. It used to taste like cinnamon. It now just tasted like... well, I'll get to that. I dreamed about polishing the hood of the car I don't have, and imagined having money to go to the bar for a beer.

But I wasn't old enough for that, either. I'm 20.

I asked myself what I was doing here. I wanted to tell myself that I was full of shit and was just dreaming when I thought I heard Jason say, "You wanna to wrestle?"

It wouldn't be such a hard question. I was on the wrestling team and so was he. I know he's a few weight classes above me. Shit, he's 185 pounds of hard weaponry. He's crushed just about everyone in the Big Seven.

I'm the little guy on the team at a whole 125 pounds. I can stand in the shade of his pecs. I've never tried, but I bet I could. Now I'm muscled hard, too. I like it and I feel good about it. I'm not weird about being the little guy. But Jason's a big guy. He would wrestle me and catch me and crush me.

I wouldn't mind, really.

He just happened to have asked after he caught me looking at his picture.

Well, it wasn't just his picture. He was nude in the picture. Shawn, the photography geek from downstate, took the picture when he was working for the yearbook staff, but I bought it from Beevus. That's not his name, but it's what people call him. He just had the habit of finding the best pictures rejected on the yearbook floor and selling them to the highest bidder. I was on the yearbook staff because I had such quick access to pictures of the man I wanted. This year's crop was breathtaking.

I made sure I was cool enough to buy several of the nude cheerleader photos. Ironically, they were more expensive. I had him throw it into the pile as a bonus so I could supposedly blackmail Jason. Beevus liked that idea. He is such a pig. The cheerleaders looked good, but oh man, Jason's was the best picture ever!

The yearbook was steadily losing money. So few people bought a yearbook that it hardly mattered to anyone, anymore. I know I had friends wonder why I tried to fit layout duties into my schedule and training. This was the coolest place to get pictures. I had no idea why Jason liked it. He had to know about the pictures.

Jason was flashing a double biceps pose and his sparkling smile to the camera. His cock was semi-hard and looked thick. The muscle on his body was incredible. His torso had a hard-sculpted look. He was showing off in the shower. Water ran down his smooth torso in sheets.

I just wanted him to fuck me.

Okay, no one's ever done that to me before. I don't even know if I like that. I think I want to like it. So, I just wanted him to hold me.

Maybe just touch me.

Okay! I don't know what I want him to do! But whatever it is, I want him to do it much nearer to me than he is now!

I don't know what I'm so upset about. Jason didn't even flinch when he saw the photo. I mean, it wasn't like he didn't know the picture existed. He was more amused that I was in the film storage room with a jar of Vaseline jerking my meat while I was staring at the picture.

I mean, he just burst into the utility room at the yearbook and began to rifle through drawers for something when he finally noticed me reassembling myself in the corner. He just stared at me, continuing the same rhythmic gum chewing he came in with, and never changed his expression. He looked at me. He looked at his picture. He looked at me. Then he resumed looking through the drawers, still chewing.

"You got a nice piece of meat," he finally said, in all seriousness. "I like that picture too."

I began to apologize and tell him it wasn't what he thought. He smiled. He was wearing one of those sleeveless T-shirts slit down the sides. His arms and lats were marble showing through with his every move.

"Whatever, Nick," he said. "You ever want to wrestle me...private style with some different rules...just say the word. By the way, where are the three prong adapters these days. I need one."

"You need a three prong adapter?" I just repeated.

"Yeah, real bad." He said with the dirtiest smile I ever saw on a guy. He jerked his hips forward just to punctuate the dig. "Doesn't everybody?"

I opened a drawer and handed it to him without taking my eyes off him. He grabbed it and headed out of the room. He suddenly stopped and turned. His warm hand grabbed the sides of my mouth and pulled my jaw open. He pulled out his gum and popped into my mouth. "Keep this for me, will ya?"

He closed my mouth. I just chewed automatically. "It's like kissing me, but the flavor lasts and lasts..."

I just stared at the door as he closed it and left. It tasted like cinnamon then. And it tasted like him. I shot in my pants at the first taste.

So we had practice as usual that afternoon; then I waited for him. I was so off-balance I knew I wasn't going to be very good at talking. I knew that. I waited for two eternities before I actually paid attention to that little voice in the back of my head- not the one muttering 'you're crazy', but the one telling me something was wrong. It was the quieter voice, saner, and when I finally listened I went inside to see what was keeping him.

The first voices I heard were chilling. "So faggot, show me how you tell a guy you want to fuck him..." I didn't recognize the voice. But the reply was unmistakable. "Fuck you dork...hhhhuuuugh!" That was Jason and he was in trouble.

I couldn't see much with the lockers in the way. I eased the door shut and lay on the floor. I remembered this was how I could watch every move my sister made. She never looked down.

I peered around the corner to see two big guys, football types, I guessed. They were easily 50 pounds heavier than Jason. Muscled bodies, short cropped black hair. One had a mustache cut real thin. It looked dorky on such a huge guy.

They held Jason in a double hammerlock; his arms turned behind him and kept him on his knees. The clean-shaven guy pulled Jason's chin back with one hand, turning Jason's head to one side hard. Jason just had a jock strap on and shreds of a T-shirt left. There was a third man standing in front of Jason. I guess he was the one that just gave Jason the gut shot that made him grunt so loud.

"Awwww, everyone knows wrestlers are just faggots. Roll around with sweaty guys, get on top...you know man." This guy was nasty. He looked like a pretty-boy suntan jock. I never had seen him before. He stood around 6'4" and was solid and ripped. Blond hair flowed down his back over a white t-shirt. He was in tight-waisted blue jeans. For some reason he didn't like Jason.

"You are gonna give me service little man," said the blond guy. He pressed his crotch into Jason's face. "Just a little suck..." He was grinding his hips.

I know Jason's a great friend and a teammate, but this was one of the hottest things I've ever seen. The blond guy had the biggest thighs. I had no idea how he kept them in any pants. Those legs were a powerful frame for that basket. The biker boots made a nice accent to this man's powerful appearance. Seeing Jason forced to suck him was more than I could quietly watch.

Jason looked furious, his face was red. "Oh man, you can do it. You want me. Everyone says so." He pushed his crotch into Jason's face again.

Jason slipped his chin free and made his best shot at a head butt.

By the sound this blond guy was making, you'd think he had his nuts rammed into the next county. I could see that Jason only brushed by him. I'm sure it was more startling on the receiving end, but I know I get worse treatment every practice.

The guys behind Jason rained punches on his head and body. The guy with the mustache slipped loose the hammerlock and put a reverse choke lock around Jason's throat. The other guy moved in front to hammer some kicks into Jason's midsection. He was kicking so hard, Jason's hips would lift upward. His knees would leave the floor on the real hard ones.

But Jason made no sound.

The clean-shaven dude pulled Jason's chest and shoulders back with the choke hold. The mustached guy slammed into Jason's guts with a huge fist. His whole arm flexed when he hammered. Jason might've made some sound under this pounding but he had no wind from the choke.

After three slams in his rippling abs, Jason finally slipped his legs from under himself and tried to kick the guy punching him. He missed wildly. The mustached dude just straddled Jason's right thigh holding him in place.

Jason ignored him and fought for breath. With his hands free, he pulled the choking arm from his throat using the other guy's pinkie like a pull-tab.

He took two deep breaths. They didn't last long. With unreal speed, the guy that was choking Jason threw himself backward and flashed his legs around his neck. Jason tried to stop him but got another slam into his guts. The guy behind him locked in a figure-four head scissors.

With deadly trouble behind already, the man in front slipped his left hand behind Jason's back holding his body in place and slapped his right hand over his abs sinking an abdominal claw into those fabulous muscles.

Jason groaned and thrashed under the combined torture. The mustached guy leaned in deep, pressing his powerful fingers into Jason's suffering torso. Jason pulled at the clawing hand to get the hold off him. The head scissors was holding him down so he couldn't roll out of the claw.

Even in this world of hurt, Jason kept his head. His face was stern with resolve. He wasn't giving up.

The blond guy was done wailing and recovered. He was standing again, face red. "You need some manners, boy." He said. "I know we used to hang together in the old neighborhood, but I can bury you with a clear conscience." He knelt next to Jason as he struggled to get free from the smothering torture of the blond guy's muscle goons.

"You have forgotten your roots," he said. "I will remind you. You are my employee. You will suck who I tell you to. You will fuck who I tell you to. You will do whatever I tell you to. If you wish to be free of this arrangement, you will go through the necessary steps that are known to you."

Jason's struggles lessened and he looked vacant. He was blacking out. "Ease up Mike," the blond said to the man head-scissoring Jason. He let Jason breathe a bit but kept his muscular legs in place. "Did you understand what I told you?" the blond man asked.

"Yes," Jason managed. The mustached guy dug his claw in deeper and Jason howled, "AAaaaaauuugh!"

"You missed a point," the blond man said. "Ease up so he can worship me properly.

"Yes, my patron," he managed through gritted teeth.

I could see that I really knew nothing about Jason's private life. I wanted to help him, but I knew someone as small as I am would just get crushed in there. I sat quiet and waited.

"Good man," the blond said, reaching into the tangle of bodies to mess up Jason's hair. "So what's it gonna be? You still with us, or are you splitting away?"

The goons on him waited for the answer. "I'm splitting away, Carl." He said with as much dignity as he could. I couldn't believe the courage. Man, he was in a world of hurt and still stood by his guns.

The blond guy stood and lit a cigarette. "Make him remember this, Dominick."

The mustached guy released the claw and punched hard. Jason's eyes snapped open as he cried out in pain. He tried to fend off the next punches but was visibly weary from the beating. Each punch hit solidly. This just seemed to go on forever.

Jason moaned with each breath. That was when Carl, the big blond threw his cigarette. He pushed Mike and Dominick aside. They let go of Jason. He pulled Jason into a sitting position and grabbed his head with both hands. He effortlessly slid into a sitting position next to Jason, hauling him bodily in between his huge legs. Jason found himself wrapped in a titanic body scissors. Already beaten and suffering, he was caught in a finishing trap. This was just insult. I knew Jason could stand any torture this guy could deliver alone.

Carl's ankles crossed at Jason's side. He straightened his legs.

Jason's pummeled and clawed gut was now being constricted and squeezed, his ribs bending under the pressure. Jason pushed at the huge legs surrounding him. They didn't move.

I could see the striation in Carl's muscled thighs press through his denim. Those legs were at least 36 inches in diameter, bigger than my waist by a lot. He was frighteningly huge.

Jason writhed in the relentless squeeze. There was no passion in Carl's face at all. Just business. "You will pay me back half of the money you have received over the past four years," He flexed his legs tighter. Jason's whole muscular frame flexed to fend off the squeezing pressure. Frantically he took a swing at Carl's face.

Dominick was on him in a flash. Resistance was not going to be tolerated. Dominick twisted Jason's arm behind him in a hammerlock and chicken winged the other. The squeeze continued and so did Carl's threats. "You will pay me back in one year's time." Jason just squirmed in Dominick's arms.

"What do you say?" Dominick demanded.

"Yes patron," Jason said his face still red with pain and anger.

Carl released him. Jason took his first real breath in five minutes. Dominick held him face down on the floor. Jason went still. Dominick hauled him to his knees again. Mike stood nearby, ready to jump in. He smiled confidently.

"Now," said Carl, standing before Jason like before. "You could do it for me, for old time's sake?" He pressed his crotch into Jason's face again. This time, I didn't appreciate it one bit. I noticed I was shaking. He was lucky I didn't have a gun just then.

"I need you, Jason, please..." Carl said in a mocking tone. Mike just burst out laughing. The locker room echoed with their laughter.

Suddenly, Jason snapped free. He was so fast, I didn't see it all. Dominick was staring at his empty hands. Carl just screamed when Jason lunged on him. With his strong right hand, he grabbed the blond guy by the balls and dragged him to the floor. His left hand was a blur of punches to his face. Well aimed punches at that. I heard his nose break. I saw his eye get smashed hard.

The others were on Jason like dogs, kicking him and beating him. Jason flattened himself onto Carl's chest and sunk his teeth into his nearest pec muscle. Carl just screamed and squirmed. No matter what they did, Jason didn't let go of the blond guy's crotch. His teeth and hand were locked in like a pitbull.

I had enough. I know I weigh almost nothing, but these guys were hurting him and there was a real fight happening. I launched off the floor and grabbed the tallest one by the hair to pull him down. The aim was good and his head hit the floor. *SPLAT!*

He stayed. I was pleased.

The other kept kicking Jason. I guess I wasn't real enough for him. His world must not have many surprises, I guessed. I sprung off the floored giant and tackled the other one. That didn't go as well.

It was Dominick. He rolled on the way down and landed on me. I felt the wind rush out of me. I tried to scramble out from under him but he closed his huge arms around me from behind. Muscular boas tightened around me. I knew I was too horny for words about then. Even though I knew I might be in trouble, his warm muscular arms sinking a hold around me was intense. I was erect in a second. Then he squeezed.

Oh man, I was in trouble. He squeezed me and laid his entire weight on me. I was blacking out. That was more than I was ready for.

Then suddenly his hold went slack. He was still on me like a lead blanket, but I knew I could get out. I rolled over to see Jason in his jock strap holding the blonde's Harley boot like a hammer. He picked me up and hugged me gently.

"You were right on time," he said, panting. His right eye was already beginning to swell. But he had this huge smile on. He was drenched in sweat from the battle and smelled so...I don't know. He smelled like I wanted to stay close to him forever. He looked in my eyes and he knew what I was thinking. I mean he really knew. He next said. "We have to leave. Then we'll get right back to this hold." He slightly tightened his hug around me.

I gave him the sweatshirt I had on over my T-shirt. He pulled it over his head and flashed that ripped row of abdominal muscles. I could see he was already bruising up. He settled into a sweatshirt obviously just too small. He didn't care and walked into the night. He had to feel the cold breeze. All he had on was my sweatshirt and a shredded jockstrap.

I numbly followed.

We climbed into his trashy Chevette. It smelled like sweat, like a rolling gym locker. Not like it was old and rotting; just like MAN. It made me stiff. I had to re-belt myself so I didn't hurt my cock.

I had no idea how this thing still rolled. It made grinding noises that didn't seem to concern Jason in the slightest bit.

The car shot a report across the commuter parking lot as he parked. In that loud silence that followed he stared at me. His breath was a fine simple sound. He looked at the keys in his hands and seemed a bit shy and unsteady.

"Would you like to have sex with a man you knew had been used by other people for money?" He said to his hands.

"You passed the HIV test for the team slot, didn't you?" I asked.

"Yeah," he said. "But..."

I was feeling a bit charged with adrenaline. My life has been bland compared to this night. I was emboldened by his shame.

"Jason, get something straight," I started. "I have never had sex with anyone. Never. Never ever!"

"Okay," he said, staring at me.

"I want you to teach me this and I know you'll be gentle about it. Shit, I don't care where the experience comes from as long as, well... ummm..." My bravado faded with the adrenaline as I sputtered into silence.

He smiled a wicked smile. Then he flashed a wicked grin.

We opened the door and turned on a light. It was a normal dorm room in most respects, but with mats on the floor. I was relieved to see he had a place where we could be mostly alone without his bloated drunk roommate asking questions. He kicked on the heat and pulled out a book light. When he turned out the main lights, the book light made a romantic glow, just enough to see him.

He eased the sweatshirt over his head showing off that body. I just realized I was so dazed that I completely failed to notice him in just a jockstrap besides the shirt. "Please take off your shirt." He said to me, slowly walking toward me with a smile.

I elbowed the wall and gave myself a rope-burn with the collar of my T-shirt I was so fast. He walked to me and I could feel his warm skin inches from me. He slowly moved his arms around me, without touching. I was surrounded by him before he touched me, I could feel the heat from his muscular body. Lightning! Our chests touched. I wrapped my arms around him and buried my face in his chest.

Like a takedown, his arms surrounded my torso and he just walked me to a reclined position. I held onto his neck and those thick traps, and I just fell to the floor in slow motion with him settling over my torso.

"Now, I'm going to touch you," he said. I almost laughed at the strange comment. He touched me so much right now, he'd have to be inside me to touch me any more. Instantly, my cock was erect. I was so hard the damn thing hurt. I wanted him to touch me. He placed his hand over my right pectoral. Gentle, warm caresses, like his fingers were just finding me, all the way to my stomach. An open hand spread over my stomach. "Nice," he said.

"Have you ever had anyone touch you here," he asked, slipping his hand gently around my cock, surrounding it in his warmth. I shook my head. "Then you'll like this." He gently touched behind my nuts, like a tickle, but softer. I was so ready. "Don't you shoot..." he warned. It took everything in my control to keep from blowing his hand off. I was so hard I felt like I was shooting already. I dribbled on his hand.

He tasted it and smiled.

He rolled onto his back carrying me on top of him. He shifted his legs and maneuvered my ass toward his hard cock. He pulled my face to his and kissed. Stubble scraped across my cheek and his mouth tasted like the gum I chewed for days. I was so close...

He reached his hand behind my nuts and found that spot again. I swear the lights dimmed in the room. "You may fire when ready." With that, he pressed behind my balls on a place I didn't even know existed. It was like I came for days. My hips lifted from the floor and every muscle went rigid. I shot clear over my head and hit the wall behind me. Then I shot six more times covering my chest and abs.

By the time I recovered, I felt Jason lifting my legs. He pressed his hard cock into my ass and slowly moved around. He massaged my hole gently with his cock. "You will enjoy this more if you don't clench." He pressed into me just an inch. Oh man, that was a fiery burn. It took him nearly ten minutes to enter me. He used lube and a condom and pressed slowly.

In time he was slowly thrusting into me. I held his muscular body tightly, wrapping my legs around him. He gently touched my calf muscles and thighs, seriously grooving on my legs. "I want you on top of me," I said.

He turned me over and propped a pillow under my crotch. His hands felt so clean and powerful, just moving me around to suit his desire. He straddled his body over mine like he was about to do a set of push-ups. He slowly entered me again, that hard cock of his penetrating my hole. I found I could relax quickly to pull him inside me. His muscular body covered mine. His hands drove under my armpits and grabbed my wrists. I felt surrounded by his body heat and smelled his breath. He chewed on my neck and traps gently and I found myself rock hard erect again.

He ground his hips into a slow rhythm. "You are so hot, Nick. I'm going to pound you now," he breathed into my ear. His grip on my wrists tightened and his whole body possessed me. Growling like an animal he doubled his speed, thrusting his cock into me deeply. I saw stars at the riot of sensations I felt. It was everything I had hoped for. I wanted him to feel wonderful and held my ass up for him to keep his hammer going.

He moaned softly, and then louder. He built to the power of a driving machine and moaned with each thrust. I knew he was close to release. "I want it! Give it to me!" I shouted.

I could tell you about how he smelled when he held me. I could tell you how his breath buzzed when he slept. I could tell you about how I woke several times with him gently running his hands over my body, how they were so warm and broad, and so strong. I could tell you we never did this again after that night.

And telling you all that can't make a dent in the reality of having it. Forever would have been too short in his arms...

He roared when he came and I felt the floor shake. He filled me with a liquid heat while the muscular power of his body nearly crushed me into unconsciousness.

I woke the next morning on my side, curled onto his chest, on the same mat. He apparently got pillows and a blanket. We really didn't need it much seeing his body turned the heat in the room up to a wasteful excess. I must've fallen asleep in his arms. He had a cool wet towel that he used to wash me. I heard the sounds of water dribbling as he rinsed it.

I never knew waking up could be so nice. He had a cool musk scented powder he covered me with, very lightly. "That's nice," I said.

"You know how many guys look like waterfowl in the morning?" he asked.

"Well, no, I don't," I said.

"It's alarming," he said and flashed a smile. "I do this so I don't ever look like that for a lover."

"Lover?"

He grabbed my nipple in his strong fingers and squeezed hard. I squirmed to get his grip off, "I love you, man." He let go of my nipple and kissed me deeply.

I didn't want that to end and I didn't want to believe it. I didn't want to marry him or anyone. I didn't want to leave his side for any reason. I was hoping that one of us could die just then so I wouldn't ever have to be practical and get dressed or go to class or work or face the consequences of the violence of the previous evening.

I was curious if this was love, or lust, or just plain kidlike stupidity. I felt so lucky that I could be there to hear those words. I felt so betrayed that my parents and teachers never said anything that might've even prepared me for this feeling.

I was instantly hard and rolled Jason over on his back. My cock pressed into his rock-solid abs and my hips wanted to rock without volition. I kissed his face and touched him and ate from his body like a man starved for years and years and years, to the point of denying there ever had been such a thing as food.

He was in a similar passion, hard as a rock. I never did this before, but I wanted to give back to him I took his cock into my mouth, only to have him pull gently me off, "Wait..." like a magic trick, he pulled a condom out of my ear with a flourish. Covered, I went back to the duty.

His hips bucked and muscles contracted, slapping the mat on the floor and touching my back and neck. His hips thrust forward once, hard. He came with a roar that sounded like a violent submission, like he was shouting his victory, echoing through the whole room.

He was so beautiful as he recovered from the passion of his orgasm. *Please don't tell me this has to end.* I feel hungry and would like some dinner, or was it breakfast. *Please don't tell me this ends.*

I dug my fingers deep into the muscle on his chest and squeezed. He sucked in a breath and threw his head back. He deeply enjoyed that. I squeezed his pecs tightly and he writhed gently on the mats, not trying to gain release, but clutching on his strength. I like to guess that way. I caressed the bruises he had and courageously ignored.

I couldn't find him the next day. You see, I went home to shower and get dressed and study. I worked out and didn't see him in the wrestler's gym. I went to see his room and it was empty. I caught up with Boofer, his bloated room mate and he said their room had a critical electric failure and Jason was moved to Ross Hall. But they never heard of him there.

I know he ran because there were people after him. I know he didn't tell me to keep me safe. I know he loves me and watches me. I did my laundry last week and found his shirt in the pile after I had folded it. I didn't put it there. It was his, really. You could smell him in it.

Big boys don't cry, right?

I'll keep going until he shows up. Please show up...soon.

*****

Two years later...

Barry stared at Nick over the remnants of the pizza they shared. Damn, he's such a cute fucker. Barry looked at their reflection in the front window of Mamma's Pizza, at his own broad shoulders and ripped features.

He remembered his man Dean and how fucked up Dean left him to go back to Buffalo, to his wife and four kids, leaving him at college to make dreams of how their gym would look in their dream house. And he remembered his tears when he decided that Dean wasn't coming back and he had to stop giving him space in his head, rent-free.

Damn, Nick sure was a cute little guy. Barry knew he had no chance of competing with Jason, in absentia, and wasn't going to try.

"Sorry to hear about it, man," Barry finally said. "You okay now?"

"You bet," Nick said with his usual cheer. He had the reputation on being the Dangerous Little Chipmunk, as they called him at the local kendo Dojo, happy, cheerful, fast and brutal in an attack and merciful toward surrender.

"Uh-huh," Barry said.

"Okay, I romantically kept a candle in the window for a year, decided to hate him, decided to burn him in effigy, decided to forget him..." He paused and looked out the window. "And then I decided to forgive him and remember what he gave me."

Nick gave Barry a wicked grin, the wickedest Barry had ever seen on a guy's face. "Life goes on, ya know?" His grin got bigger as he fumbled in his pocket. Barry's eyes got wide as Nick held out a packet to him.

"Gum?"

THATCH: A FAIRY TALE

For the longest time, I knew I was insane. Yes, this was long before I became a Penultimate Certified Fighter. But that was just part of the sickness. It doesn't bother me, really. I've known this a long time, since around thirteen I guess. That was when I met Thatch. Thatch was a Fairy.

No, he wasn't limp-wristed or something. He was Fey, with the body of a man and wings and everything including a healthy disrespect for clothing. He had a lean and muscular body, a handsome face and a wicked smile. He was so strong. Nothing compared to being in his arms.

And he wasn't fragile. The wings could fold down and out of the way. He wrestled like an octopus, always being where I wasn't. He would wrap me up in his muscular legs and always ask, "Had enough yet?" That was always just before he squeezed the crap out of me.

We weren't exactly friends at first. But Thatch took pity on me.

We became friends one day on the playground at Our Lady of Mount Divinity grade School. Richard Ellicot called me a fairy and Thatch told me that Richard must have very good taste to compliment me so.

I just stared at him. Just before Richard beat someone up, he always called him a fairy. Everyone knew this. Oblivious to Richard's threatening posture, Thatch did nothing. Thatch was surprised and offended when Richard proceeded to pound me in the face because he decided I was a fairy.

At that point, Thatch decided I needed a keeper.

Thatch was pissed. Indignant, even. Being a Fairy was bad? It took years until Thatch really believed the bullies meant that in a derogatory manner. He would try to dismiss each occurrence as an isolated problem. Thatch was only 145 years old then and was going to be naive for the next four hundred years. That worried his mother. He was one of the very few new Fairies born near the times of Darwin and Marx.

But that's another story.

Around that time of the playground incident, Thatch began to teach me most everything he knew. He started with fighting and sex. It seemed to be more about sex, though. By the age fifteen, little Joe, that's me, knew lots about sex, and liked it too. Most of the kids my age were not very interested in sex or maybe I just wasn't really interested in them. I was pretty pragmatic about this; most kids that know about sex at the age fifteen were really weird anyway.

Sex with male fairies? I knew I was in the strangest and most exclusive of company at that point.

I guess these were all excuses I used to justify having sex with Thatch. He made loving him easy. He listened when I talked. He held me when I was scared. It didn't seem to matter where we were. He even held my hand when we had that big science exam where we had essay questions about sexual reproduction. I was afraid I knew too much.

And no one ever saw him.

He knew just when to put his hand inside my shirt and touch my chest. He'd run his hands across my chest and kiss my neck gently, usually while he was behind me. I loved the feeling of his body running the length of me. It always made me feel horny, powerful, and safe.

Thatch would then follow me home from School and we'd take the short cut through a stand of forested land. It never turned out to be a short cut. He'd usually tackle me from behind and we'd roll down the grassy hill toward the creek. He'd pretend to be pinned by me and before I knew it I'd lose my shirt.

Then he would make his usual threats. "Man, you're gonna get squeezed now." He loved wrapping me up in some squeezer, his toughest being the body scissors. It didn't matter how hard I fought, I always landed in that bear trap. Slam, he'd close his legs around me and cross his ankles.

The long chorded muscle in his legs would stand out as he flexed, hard pressure cutting into my waist. I'd make a show of not surrendering. Squeeze after squeeze, he'd pump his legs to make hard spasms of crushing pressure. He'd crush me eventually, but I got better at surviving his assault.

By the time I was in high school, he could squeeze me and I could flex against that terrible pressure and not surrender. But he'd still wrap me up, somehow, no matter how hard I fought to defend against it.

Then he would pull me toward his face and suck my nipples and touch me everywhere. He was always so warm. I loved it when he would straddle my waist and rub his butt on my cock. When I entered him, he would spread his wings wide and softly groan. The sun through his wings was like crystal panes, so thin, yet so strong. I never saw them tear or get hurt.

Well, not until that night.

We could fuck non-stop. He had this power to keep me from cumming, milking out every moment of pleasure. Just when things began to hurt too much, he'd let me go. He sounded like a peacock when he came.

I knew my life was real weird when my mother was walking Scamp through the woods and came past Thatch and I fucking each other like a rusty well pump. I wasn't even quiet about it. She just walked on by, never even seeing us. This cemented in my mind the fact that no one could (or would) see us, I mean, if your own Mother (and her little dog, too) could walk right past and never notice the things that Father Venashkavili would personally send you to Hell for, well geez...

It really didn't faze me, though. Weird occurrences didn't bother me much after a while. Having a friend that flew into the playground every day to say Hi was a benchmark of weirdness that was hard to pass.

So Thatch and I played at sex. He could be annoying some days, though, bringing it up when it was most inconvenient. My sister's wedding was very uncomfortable as a result. Thatch crawled under the pews and reached into my pants while he was sitting and listening to Father Venashkavili deliver the sermon.

He pulled out my cock and sucked on it playfully. I knew no one would watch. They never watched anything Thatch did. (Thatch explained it was hard on their reality. They didn't believe Fairies were real. And Fairies in church? No way. "Just wait until a real

Ogre comes into their midst. Mother, they'll be sorry.")

Just to prove the point that day, Thatch sang in the choir right along with the ladies. I was afraid that he would just begin to mock the whole thing, but he didn't. It was beautiful. The whole congregation was in tears at the beautiful sound the singers made with Thatch's help. I couldn't help feeling like the luckiest guy in the world, even though I knew I was insane.

I was insane the day Kent Bradley saw Thatch. Kent was sick. He was diagnosed with Attention Deficit Disorder, but that's not what made him sick. I knew kids with ADD – they were cool mostly. But Kent was sick.

He was on the wrestling team in high school, but got kicked off for something so bad Coach wouldn't talk about it. I only knew it happened because I was staying late (yeah, Thatch again) in the gym and saw the ambulance take Johnny Mason away. I never saw Johnny again, but the next day Mrs. Bradley spent all day in the Principle's office, just her, the Principle and the Bradley's expensive lawyer. Kent didn't get back on the team but did stay in the school. Most of us hoped he would at least be expelled, maybe even killed, but no such luck.

By the time Kent saw Thatch, I was going to the Catholic Community College. I was taking my first karate classes. My mom was getting older and needed me to go to school nearby. Kent went there because nowhere else would take him and his Mom made enough donations. Okay, okay, I don't have proof of that. But I wouldn't have taken that maniac.

Kent liked to hurt things. He could always be found around the campus killing something small. He caused a small University wide controversy surrounding crucified squirrels that "died for Jesus' sins."

Well, he was proudly announced "cured" by his mother when they started giving him medication. It was explained to me (while Thatch rolled his eyes and waved his cock at Mrs. Bradley) that Kent was unable to pay attention because his brain lacked the capacity to focus. "All the medication does is help him focus," she said. "And look at him! He wouldn't hurt a fly."

I didn't believe it. I was right.

Kent was only about 5'4" tall, but he muscled up in tenth grade. By then, he had the appearance of a small ape, furry, leanly muscled and never clean.

I grew pretty well. I was over 6' tall but found wrestling in my junior year and developed a lean ripped torso with thick legs. My wrestling bouts with Thatch paid off very well. No one in the school could beat me. I always managed to miss out on the city championships though. Coach said I was too easily distracted. I don't know; Thatch usually had to work real hard to get my attention during matches. I never did take home a trophy.

Thatch and I took a habit of walking through the woods behind the library. He would hold me on the tough days and kiss me when he was feeling horny. It was late one night, just before finals. I was studying in the stacks, with Thatch's help.

I'd been at the books for hours and finally had to get some air. It seemed there was no one around. The rural Catholic College was so quiet when people were gone on break. All that could be heard was the wind. Thatch held me so close and I still really hate myself for not noticing the sound of footsteps. As he kissed me, I knew we were in trouble as I felt a sharp blow to the back of the head...

When I woke, I saw Thatch with Kent's muscular fist around his throat. He punched Thatch so many times, I lost count. Kent dropped Thatch's limp body and turned to me.

This was all wrong. I always believed that no one could ever hurt Thatch. I guess that was just the arrogance of youth, seeing as I never could.

"You guys are real funny," he said with a smile. "You think no one can see what you Fairies are doing. I didn't for the longest time, but the medication helped a lot." He kicked me in the face and I was out.

When I woke up, I heard nothing but a car starting up. I ran toward the lights and saw Kent's mom's station wagon riding away. I didn't see Thatch anywhere.

My heart was racing. I could barely breathe. I noticed that every muscle in my body throbbed with rage, or power, or something that men get when they really know they can kick ass. I had to do something.

We had never been separated for so many years it was immediately terrifying. I ran toward the station wagon, but it was speeding away. I was too dizzy to follow and dropped again. I'm not sure what happened for a while, but I know I stayed on my knees sobbing for so long. Too long.

"Son, what's wrong?" said a deep male voice. Lights surrounded me from the sheriff's car. The man's face was beautiful. He was smiling in a concerned way and sounded so gentle. I fell in his arms and felt the strength in his huge arms.

"He took my friend away. He beat us up and took him away," I was frantic. If he had been one of those blobs from the Felton's donut shop I would've said nothing.

"Tell me his name, what's your friend's name," He asked,

urgently.

"He's Thatch. They just went down County 15. We can catch them!" I got up to run...somewhere. I felt like throwing up. Warm hands surrounded my arms and lifted me. I was suddenly in the front seat of the Sheriffs cruiser and we were rumbling down the County Road.

Corn and more brown corn flew by the windows. We took quick glimpses down the access roads but saw nothing. Then we came up on Kent's wagon. It was stopped and abandoned.

"You stay in here," the Deputy said. He slowly walked up to the car with his nightstick out; no it was a flashlight. He looked into the car but apparently saw nothing. He let out a deep sigh and turned to walk back. I opened the car door. I don't know why, I just wish I hadn't.

We heard a scream.

My whole body was trembling and the world was fuzzy. I wasn't right in the head. But the world was wrong too. It was fuzzy, not my head. I could see the Sheriff look at the hanging gauzy haze in wonder. I jumped up and looked around. I couldn't see him yet, but I knew that out in one of the fields was Thatch. He screamed again. It was like music but horrible. The most pained sound in my world, but perfectly in key with the rest of the sounds of the night.

I ran. The Deputy's light sprayed my shadow around in front of me. In that weird light I saw Kent. They were by a fence. I couldn't look at Thatch yet. It was like he hung limply in mid air. I just knew he was being hurt and I was going to make it stop.

"YOU FUCKER!" I dove on Kent and hit him and kicked him and bit him. He feebly punched at me, "Dude! You didn't hear him. Man! This is wild!" Kent said, like it was a defense I would appreciate. "He makes the greatest sounds!"

The Deputy ripped me off Kent and everything was weird again. I think he hit me. It hurt and I was spitting dirt out of my mouth when I woke up.

"I told you he's a psycho," Kent said when I was waking.

"Son, why are you attacking him," I didn't see the Deputy. I didn't see Kent. I just saw a beam of light from the cruiser. It moved while I was out. The light shown on Thatch's mangled body. It looked like he was knifed a thousand times. He still moved. He was shaking and cold. I know he was cold. Don't tell me he wasn't!

I pulled myself to my knees. Kent was handcuffed. I walked over to my friend.

"Thatch?"

"Joe," Thatch said to me. "Joe, this hurts. Help me."

"Now just wait a minute," the Deputy said losing his patience. "You will answer me young man!!"

"Come here," I said through my tears. To this day, I'm sorry I did this. I'll never do it again, I swear! I took the Deputy's hand and placed on Thatch's shoulder. "This is my friend. Please help us. Please?"

I don't know whether it was Thatch's injuries, ugly violations on someone so beautiful, or suddenly having his reality irreversibly, forcibly changed to suddenly include a raped and tortured Fairy, or all of the above. He screamed and shook his hand like he was bit by something. He turned pale and screamed more. He held his head and wouldn't stop screaming. Kent added to the chaos by laughing in sick delight at the Sherriff's agony.

I knew there was no one to help, no one to stop the pain, no one to help anymore. I was wrong, but I knew it all for a fact right then.

That's when I shot Kent.

I grabbed the gun off the Sheriff. I turned on Kent. He laughed so hard at the Deputy's pain. It was pitiful. It's just a fairy and shouldn't hurt to see him. But Kent wouldn't stop laughing. I put a bullet in that sick fucker's head and I'm still not sorry.

The Deputy still screamed and then he ran. His anguish trailed off into the night, leaving me alone with a pain there was no running from.

"Thatch?"

"There... you... are." I lifted him off the barbed wire as gently as I could. He tried to speak but just whimpered.

"I'm here," I said. "How did he hurt you? I could never do this."

"I'm...so glad," he said. His smile was still rakish and seductive. "Hate will do this. I know you can't hurt me. That's why I stayed. But the others..."

"I love you, Thatch," I said. I meant it.

"You're just saying that because you know I have to leave now..."

I couldn't take the idea of him dying. Tears made the light blurry and even worse. I couldn't see. Then there was someone else there.

"Thatch Furious Flash," It was a woman. It was obviously a mother – only mothers use three names for their children when they're really pissed.

"Mom?" he said, so plaintive. I bet I sounded like that when I skinned my knee.

"Come home, dear," she said again.

"Coming," he said. Against all reason, he stood and walked out into the field where we heard the voice come from.

"Can't he ever come back?" I begged. I felt selfish, but so lonely already I had to ask.

Then the most beautiful woman ever living appeared. I know I'm supposed to say it that way. But you would believe me. She shone like stars and loved me. I knew it.Right to my bones I knew it "Thatch has to get better before he can go anywhere, child." She touched my face and, just for a moment, I believed it was going to be just fine.

"How long?" I asked.

"He'll come back," She said. She looked at Kent's messed up body. She shook her head. "Tsk child! This fixes nothing." I felt so ashamed I wanted to sink into the dirt. "You need people to know we all live together. This can only set us back!"

"I'm sorry, Ma'am."

"Not yet," she said. I knew she was right. "Let me take this. His Mother will miss him, but she'd earned other blessings worse than this." Kent's body sank into the ground like a rock into mud.

"The soldier you call Sheriff will be right as the Moon in a little while," She said. "Most people make themselves forget us. I suggest you try it." With that she kissed my cheek and walked off into the field.

****

I never knew the name of the Deputy that was there that night. No one knew I was there and I didn't tell anyone. I never felt bad about killing Kent until I thought about Thatch. I knew he could be seen and it was arrogance that made me think I was the only one that ever could see him.

The years went by and I was going to make sure this never happened again

****

I could hear the announcer's voice in the auditorium. "Oh, Joe's getting hammered! How can a fighter take this much abuse and keep standing!"

That was when I was sure I was losing this fight. "The Polygon has never seen such punishment of a single fighter!" The ref pulled "Sooper Pig" Ham Leinster off me. He came from the Florida Pit-Fighter schools. He was short with huge legs and stout limbs, impossible to knock over. I knew from the start I'd have to be faster. But he hammered me a couple times and pounded my eye a few more. I was getting a hundred little bruises, mostly from body shots.

I'm still not sure why they had an announcer. This was part of that pro-wrestling middle ground that the penultimate fighting group evolved out of. The guy was so annoying telling the screaming fools about something pretty obvious happening in the pit. The crowds these days were so accustomed to hearing someone telling them what they were seeing that they couldn't grasp it without an announcer. At least it wasn't a laugh-track.

I was dazed and not sure why they put us back at the draw position. I stood, ready to guard myself. Lester rushed me burying his shoulder in the pit of my stomach. I landed on my back hard and he straddled me to mount.

I knew I took him by surprise when I kicked into a bridge so hard I flipped him clean over my head and followed along. The training I did on my bridge paid off. Instead of laying on the ground with him pounding on me, we landed with me on top of him and he had to scramble.

He slapped his thick legs around my waist and screwed them tightly in place around me. His guard was a well-known dangerous place to be. I was trapped between his legs with him on his back. With a shift of his weight, he would be able to move quickly into a number of submission holds that all suck. He immediately moved to find an elbow lock, his near-famous crippler maneuver.

I tried to pull my arm away and found he had it tightly wrapped in his muscular hands, like a fisherman slowly pulling his catch in closer, he was working to slip some leverage behind the elbow. His brown eyes sparkled as he saw I was trapped. Figures. He liked crippling people.

The basics still worked, when pull fails you push. I shoved my whole arm deep into his hold to press my elbow beyond his leverage point. To make the move that more interesting, I aimed my right elbow toward his face.

The elbow shot split his eyebrow and rocked his head backward. Blood mixed with the sweat on his face and the crowd howled in appreciation, but he never lost that sparkling smile. His short-cropped hair stood in sweaty spikes.

Missing the point, I guess, I found out why he let in the shot. My ribs were instantly on fire. His armlock bit deeply into my right bicep as he flexed those powerful thighs and muscled the air right out of my lungs. I thought I could take everything a guy could dish out with just a scissors hold.

I slammed my forehead into his nose, twice, three times! Damn! He wouldn't let go. I was getting the breath crushed out of me and I didn't think any of these guys could do that. I flexed hard trying to force some room to breathe.

I pushed on the Pig's legs even with the crappy leverage I had. He held my left arm and wasn't giving it back. To make it hurt that one bit more, he slipped his hand over my left and bent my wrist against my chest. I could tell right away that the human wrist was not meant to go that way. Pain shot clear up to my elbow and I could feel everything in my wrist stretch.

The sweat and blood we shared let me slip my wrist back into a working position but distracted me thoroughly. In one quick motion, he pushed me away from his chest and coiled his legs around my neck and left shoulder, like a scissors choke, he cut off my breath, but did so my wrenching my shoulder into my ribcage. There was nothing, no air at all.

I felt myself slip onto my back, the crowd roar sounding like static on an empty television channel, loud at first but trailing off to a rushing silence. Leinster's wicked smile burned into my eyes. *He should really save the wicked shit for someone who cares.* It was all I could muster to even think the thought.

Danny, my trainer pulled me off the sand covered floor. I felt myself being hauled back through the weight rooms to the showers. I think I lay on my bench for ten minutes before agreeing to move.

By then, the next match was well under way.

I sat up and looked in the mirror. My left eye was bleeding. My head looked swollen in a number of places. But, damn! I still looked good. Tight muscular body, hard and compact. Thick quads and a neck that was framed by deep traps and shoulders. Even if I got my ass kicked tonight, it was better than years before.

In the mirror I could see spots that were blurry in the background. I dismissed it as the usual stuff that happens when you get your head pounded on a lot.

"But you don't have to get your head pounded in any more," a voice said behind me.

I turned so fast everything hurt. It was Thatch. I had turned to see an empty space so many times in the last ten years the reality didn't register for a minute. After all, headshots can mess you up for a while...

Just in case, I tried to look casual, like I expected him all this time. I rehearsed this look so many times; you'd think I could pull it off. But I had forgotten just how magical Fairies really are.

He was beautiful.

He had grown. His chest was larger with a chase of downy black hair covering his pecs. His abs were ripped, he was in terrific shape. His wings had taken on a greenish blue color. They were about as long as his body was tall. I guess his shoulders and lats were the most impressive. It takes muscle to get those wings to work.

He had no scars. I felt tears ran down my cheeks when I noticed that. He hadn't been disfigured by Kent's sick mutilations. I would've hated myself if he were.

Shit, I didn't think much of me anyway.

"You look impressed," Thatch said.

"I am... you're beautiful."

"Thanks. I've been flying a lot. Great cardio workout. Safer than yours, I might add." He looked at me. "You look like walking is too much work right now. Never mind flying."

Just then my agent came in, looking all over for me. I almost called his name as he walked between Thatch and me into the showers and back. "Same old people," Thatch said. "They just can't."

He walked over to me and touched my shoulder. I was shaking, trying not to cry. "I'm sorry." I said. "I wish I could've helped. Back then. You know."

"Oh Joe," he said and kissed my forehead. I wrapped my arms around his torso. He was like hugging warm stone. "I'm all right. I spent the last ten years healing and I'm better than ever. Mom told me she said that to you. Didn't you believe her?"

"I didn't know her," I was in full sobs now. "I wanted to but I missed you and I was afraid..."

He just stared at me in astonishment. "I spent ten years getting stronger and you spent them feeling guilty?" There was an anger in his voice that hurt badly. He slapped me in the face. "DUMB-ASS!"

He cut to the quick of the matter. "And look at you, all that training you had from all those teachers in fighting is useless, sitting on the crumbling ruins of your confidence. At first you were fighting to learn strength, now you're just looking for someone to punish you properly for getting me raped and nearly killed!"

"IT'S NOT MY FAULT!" I screamed back.

He paused for the echo of my noise to die down. "I know that you poor asshole...you're the one who doesn't believe it." He looked at me with painful intensity. "Not for one second, all these years. You didn't forgive yourself for one second."

I fell into his arms, sobbing. Strangely, his voice was softer, "Hey, Dude, It's Ok. You didn't do anything wrong... It's all Ok now... Really... It's all Ok..." He stroked my hair and held me in his warm, gentle arms. "Please believe it now."

As I wept out a decade's worth of guilt and loneliness in the haven of his arms I began to believe that maybe, just maybe, he was right. Everything will be fine.

I must have said something like that, or maybe he had gotten better at reading my mind in Fairy school.

"I am gonna have SO much fun proving it to you over the next century or so.." he whispered in my ear, his warm breath caressing me again. As I felt his lips brush my neck it was as though the last ten years just melted away, and everything was right in the world again.

That's when Leinster walked into the locker room, took one look at us, screamed like a girl and fainted dead away. "Hmmm," said Thatch, thoughtfully. "Maybe the world is changing..."

MARK'S RETURN
THE PRODIGAL

The queue point was sharply outlined by laser-banded beams keyed to alarm when crossed. Adam stood still. This was not a hardship, considering the number of times he's had to queue to vouch for someone landing at the Sonny Bono Terminal. The Command told him this would be different than most diplomatic assignments and might be real tough. He couldn't take his mind off the quiet compliment underlying the fact that they sent him to do the hard jobs.

Of course they send the best for the hard jobs. He tried not to remember that they also sent the disposable people to do the impossible jobs.

The war with the Tredorans was not going well. The world Union declared the war hoping that the occupation on the mineral rich huge planet would go quickly. What the world Union would gain in uranium, platinum, gold, silver, and diamonds, would make them galactic powers.

It was true that the Tredorans had no military.

It was true that they were hardly organized.

It was also true that Tredor was a planet with gravity three times stronger than that of Earth, making the native population terrifyingly strong and hard to kill. On top of that problem, Terrans had never conducted a military operation in gravity stresses higher than 2.2g. The Tredoran religion that united the people of Tredor served as the closest thing they had to a government. The negotiations with them to end the conflict were going strangely.

The Terran delegation was not interested in converting to a lizard based philosophy that worshiped warming yourself on a hot rock and contemplating peace while working out to make yourself as muscular as possible. The Tredoran delegation just plain didn't understand what the invasion was about and wouldn't proceed until some common ground was achieved.

There was only one known Terran that had any extended association with the Tredorans, a wrestler from the Orion Olympic Team that took an "internship" with the Tredorans after getting beaten to shit in a PWA sanctioned match. Initially, the Planetary Wrestling Alliance called the move a kidnapping. After a few half-hearted attempts to communicate with the Tredorans, the issue was dropped and Mark Kowalski was almost forgotten.

There were no Vids of the match released – not that there wasn't interest. The people of Earth were keenly interested in seeing how a human fared against a Tredoran. They theorized that the Tredorans suppressed the Vid because it showed one of their best getting his ass kicked.

But we all know better, Adam thought.

The Terran was beaten so badly and humiliated so thoroughly that most men in Planetary Intelligence couldn't watch. But they showed the Vid to the Diplomatic newbies regularly just to see who in the Force really liked watching, for documenting future sexual aberrations among the agents.

The Tredoran Shuttle docked on time to the second. After a pause, the airlock opened and a man stepped through. Even through the travel suit, Adam could see that this man was freakishly huge. Massive as opposed to tall. He walked slowly, about half the speed most people on a schedule would. He walked up to Adam and took off his helmet. "Mark Kowalski, Terran, Oklahoma City. Requesting permission to return to Earth."

"Adam Flint," Adam said extending his hand. He expected a crushing grip but was surprised by a warm muscular hand delivering a deliberate and gentle clasp. "I'm here to vouch for you. I'm from Planetary Intelligence and would like to welcome you to Earth."

Mark's face smiled. He was tanned and handsome. His appearance was stunning. His eyes had turned silver and reflected light. His hair, formerly blond, was a silvery blue and shifted in hue like fish scales. His body was deeply muscled. "Thank you, Adam," Mark said. "I understand you've taken personal risks in vouching for my safety here on Earth. I thank you very much. It's good to be here."

Adam smiled. "At PI we take some risk vouching, but it's different for civilians. Lots of checks. They already know everything about me so the checks amount to merely reading my file." Gambit number one, tell the returning muscle-hulk that Planetary Intelligence personally vouched for him. "To business, are you acting as an agent for the Tredoran government or have you ever acted in that capacity?"

"Shit, no," Mark said smiling. "They have no government. I'm not a spy either nor will I tell them the color of the sky." He sank into a conspiratorial whisper. "It's still blue, isn't it?"

"Yes sir, it's still blue." Adam said. "Pardon the questions; they are nearly a ritual formality. Just asked to make sure you don't hurt anyone here."

"And who would stop me?" Mark said with a smile.

"I would, Mr. Kowalski," Adam said evenly.

"Wow," Mark said quietly. "You must be real good. Ever fight a Tredoran?"

"No, I haven't," Adam said, shifting uneasily. "But I think you know that. Your unique position in history is taken up with your claim that you've fought Tredorans in hand to hand combat and won."

Mark's eyes seemed to glow as he met Adam's. Adam felt a rush like he had just gone down the first hill of a roller coaster; quick, then done. He suddenly took the conversation three questions and answers beyond where they were. "Oh, sure. I'll teach you. Tonight?"

Adam nearly sputtered. "Teach me what?"

"How to fight like a Tredoran," Mark said.

He was supposed to just deliver this guy to Command and not handle this combat himself. They would get someone else involved . He was sure not interested in getting beaten, pinned, and fucked by this monster.

Mostly not interested. Almost not interested.

He was really sure this was all unplanned and not what was supposed to happen. He was really sure that he would hate himself if he didn't at least touch this man. He didn't have to tell anyone.

"Tonight? I'm sure there are introductions we have to..."

"Adam, understand this, I desire being with you too," Mark said. "And that's okay. We'll work something out. Where to next?" The Man's casual acceptance was even more unnerving than his amazing appearance.

Adam was shaken already. Here he was, four minutes into their first contact with this guy, and they were hot on their way to having sex. *I don't fuck guys!* Adam quietly argued to himself, conveniently ignoring the base urges he'd fought all his life. Command had no idea what this guy was like.

* * *

Major Mitchell looked at the recording of the meeting with the returning wrestler. He froze the frame and got a sharp close-up on Mark's face. "Why are his eyes like that?" He asked his staff who were sitting around the table.

"The Tredoran sun is intense and their diet gives them plenty of melatonin boosters – his skin is tanned," said his science tech, Ms. Brown. She moved to the Philadelphia facility from the Strategy Service in Nigeria. Known for blunt talk and taking no shit, Ms. Brown chose PI, they did not choose her. "Their diet is rich in dissolved heavy metals. His eyes are probably some side effect of mild poisoning. If I were to diagnose him from this picture, i'd say he's probably suffering metal poisoning of some sort. I have no idea why the hair is like that. The only procedure we have on earth like that involves tropical fish DNA replacement. Southeast Asian beauty schools were getting models to make their hair a permanent blue or green with tropical fish enzyme replacements in their hair."

"Okay," said the Major. "So they made him a gay freak. Marvelous. Dispose of him now."

"I'm sorry sir," said a pasty Lieutenant in a badly pressed uniform. "Command wants to know how to defeat the Tredorans. We need to know what The Prodigal knows first."

"He's a goddamn faggot telepath!" the Major snapped. "He's shown me everything I need to know. To defeat the Tredorans, you need to become a muscle-bound faggot. And that's bullshit, by the way!"

The nameless Lieutenant quickly looked down at his desk breaking eye contact but quickly composed himself. The Major didn't even look at the depth of the rebuke he delivered. Everyone else saw he was cut to the bone. "Yes sir," he said eventually. The Major, caught up in his own egotistical, multifaceted bigotry, also missed the measured look Ms. Brown was giving him.

"I'll take any heat that comes from command about this," the Major continued. "This is a dead man. Do you all understand me?"

The chorus of agreement filled the room and people filed out. Except Ms Brown. She adjusted her suit coat and stood in front of the Major. "Was there something, Ms. Brown?" the Major asked. He was a tall man towering about a foot over Ms. Brown.

"Just following orders," she said. "You remember the order you gave me after the Wilson incident where you ordered me to tell you when you're being dangerously stupid?. I am activating that privilege now."

"Okay, Brown," the Major ran his hand through his stubby hair. "I want to know what's so valuable about this man."

"Firstly, we didn't become Communists when we spied on the Russians and used their science," her long red fingernails kept score for the Major as she listed these details. "Secondly, we're the good guys and don't go killing people that aren't useful to us. Thirdly, it will look curiously like a muscular alien tainted fag threatens you in some deep part of your personal security. Don't go measuring dick-size with the hulk. It makes you look frail to the Promotion Review Board, even if you turn out to be bigger."

"Yes ma'am," he said, without looking her in the eyes. "Let the others know that I want some tactical plan to get useful information out of this monster and then isolate him from further disturbances. Tell Sergeant Flint that he's the babysitter until we have a team to relieve him. Start with sightseeing and work out some way to use your time."

"You know they're gonna fight and Flint is going to be crushed or... um, used?" Brown had a nervous smile to go with the comment.

"Flint is disposable," the Major said. "If Kowalski hurts him, we can send him through the criminal track and that will take of our isolation problem." He put his hat on.

"One more thing," Brown said. "Replace staff Lieutenant Kirk."

"Why is that?" Mitchell asked.

"If you're going to witch-hunt, be thorough in your witch-hunting. He's gay and really resents your characterization of the Prodigal," Ms. Brown said meeting Mitchell's gaze. "You didn't notice his reaction to your mouthy outburst? He was really cut by that. Even if he was going to work out, you don't have an ally there right now."

"Why are you telling me this?" Mitchell asked.

"I'm doing my job, sir. I don't like all of it, but who does?" she said. "He'd be a fine member of the team, but now, he's been polarized against you. I don't want to clean up after it."

"We've been over this..."

"Yes we have," she said. "We are not talking about your stone-age views on sexuality. We're talking about politically surviving your little outburst. Nothing more."

"Understood. And Ms. Brown?"

"Yes, sir?" she said at casual attention.

"You were very gentle. Thank you for saving my career," he said evenly.

"You're welcome sir," she said and turned to leave. She left the office and rounded the corner. *You're welcome for now, you moron. That was your one chance. Use it wisely.*

They had already gone to the tourist-like places. Even though they had clearance to visit most any place on the planet, they stayed in the vicinity of the Two Guns, Arizona facility. They had Malls, and sights, and food. They stopped for Italian food twice in a single afternoon. Adam was amazed at the sheer amount of food Mark could consume. He was used to being stared at for being able to eat. A muscular man is built out of something.

He turned on the lights and announced, "Here's my place." The simple apartment was decorated in a Japanese minimalist style. The loft had 25 foot ceilings, great for Arizona weather. There were tatami for sitting in front of floor height tables, presumably for HD complex viewing. There were several living areas, not actual rooms, dominated by open space. The flow moved at a right angle with the kitchen in the center and the bedroom at the end.

The bedroom was a thick pile tan carpet with a single king-sized futon in the center of the floor.

The only western furnishings were the computer console and a business station. Everything was clean and in place.

"Will we stay here tonight?" Mark asked.

"Um... I had the hotel in mind. There are more traditional beds there."

Mark laughed. "You have no idea what I've been sleeping on for the past ten years. Tredorans have a love for warm flat stone. This futon would be seen as a vulgar weakness only the sick and very old would find comfort in."

"I am still a nesting simian," Adam said. "I like my blankets. The rest I keep simple. I'll just pick up some things and we'll go to the hotel." Adam walked to the closet at the furthest end of the room. He stepped out of the closet...

Mark's fist hit him square in the face. Adam felt heavy hands grab the front of his shirt and haul him into the air. He flew over the futon and landed on the floor skidding toward the kitchen.

He snapped to his feet and saw Mark stripping off his shirt. His skin was remarkable and he might've been more interested in that if Mark weren't trying to kill him. His skin was tan fading to blue at the center of his torso. His chest was huge, two huge bundles of muscle tapering to a severely narrow and ripped waistline.

Adam had no idea why Mark was attacking. "Stop, what's wrong..." He scrambled to the kitchen and grabbed a chef's knife from the block and swung wildly at Mark's advancing arm. Smoothly catching the knife by the blade, Adam heard the blade snap in two as it was wrenched out of his hand.

The other meaty hand wrapped around Adam's throat and closed tightly. He was hauled close against Mark's chest. The second arm wrapped warmly over Adam's shoulder and across his chest. He found himself surrounded in warm muscle. Adam fired two quick elbows into Mark's ribcage to free himself and found that only hurt his arm. He'd never felt a man so dense with muscle. Mark's voice sounded hotly in his ear. "If you're afraid, you can not beat them. You've been told I can be dangerous at a moment's notice. I'm unstable. I'm tainted by those aliens, aren't I?"

Mark's arm flexed across his throat making Adam frantic. Adam fired a kick into Mark's instep. Hard as stone. He kicked into Mark's kneecap. More stone. *What did they turn this guy into?*

Taking breaths in huffing gulps, Adam tried to nod. His eyes were wide in shock. He debated hitting his panic button. It was a small transceiver planted in a chip under his scalp on the back of his head. The following forces would come in and intervene. Then he realized, this is Mark's first training lesson. *I can't handle this,* Adam said to himself.

"Yes, you can," Mark calmly intoned. "You already forgot? I like you. Learn from this moment. Where is your mind? Frozen! You've already lost!" Mark flexed his left arm closed across his chest. Adam felt his ribs bend, Only *one arm and he's already crushing me.*

"Don't forget, I can choke you to death," he said barely tightening his grip over his throat.

Mark then removed his arm from Adam's throat and completed his hug. Both muscular arms surrounded him warm as a furnace. "We're staying here tonight. We don't have much time and there's lots to cover."

A long pause hung in the air as Adam wondered where this went next. He was surrounded in a powerful embrace. In spite of that, Mark let Adam turn and face him. Slowly, Adam put his arms around Mark and returned the embrace. He suddenly realized he was terrified, not of this huge man, but of the government watching him.

The arms draped around him were heavy. He was wrapped around this amazing, blue-tinted torso, pressed deep into the cleft between his pectorals. He couldn't look Mark in the eye. He didn't dare ask to be released. He didn't want that. *No retreat...* He tightened his arms around Mark's granite torso and rested his face on Mark's chest. "You scared the shit out of me," Adam said.

"Good, there's too much shit in you already," Mark said softly. "But you learn fast. Rule one: physical affection is the only reassurance Tredorans understand. If you 're afraid to touch one, they will *never* trust you.

"Okay, I'm at your mercy right here," Adam said. "I like it, but this a difficult position to negotiate from."

"You should see the Tredoran Courts," Mark laughed.

"I didn't know they had a government."

"No, they don't," Mark said. "They have a mediation service preformed by their Slerns, that's a priest. It all starts by each supplicant holding the genitalia of the other." Mark released the hold and reached into Adam's crotch cupping his pack in his hand. He grabbed Adam's hand and placed on his own.

Adam looked like he was in such strange turf that he just might squeak instead of talk. "So then what..."

"Then everyone knows you came there with serious intent and mean to leave in peace or leave impotent," Mark smiled. He gently massaged Adam's crotch. "And you can tell when you have struck a friendship, too. It sort of stands out."

Adam was just getting his heart rate down to a manageable level when Mark massaged his cock. It sprang to life and he was rock hard. He couldn't believe that he could be so turned on by a man at all, let alone this much. Mark said, "Take your shirt off." Adam didn't want to. He didn't not want to. He knew where this was going. He stripped his shirt off, revealing his ripped torso and tight chest. Mark rubbed his hand over his chest, cupping his hand over his right pec. "Nice." Then Mark said, "Let's wrestle. It's fun. C'mon!" With speed that seemed unreal compared to his size, Mark wrapped a hand around Adam's thigh and slammed him on his back to the carpeted floor.

"Ugh!" Adam grunted, offering no resistance. Mark straddled him in a schoolboy pin. His massive thighs surrounded Adam's torso holding him solidly in place. Mark felt heavy and warm. Adam's hard cock rested right in between Mark's thighs. Mark moved his hips slowly over Adam's crotch, flexing his massive thighs and glutes. Adam's vision blurred he was so horny. His hips bucked into Mark involuntarily. Mark slipped an arm around Adam's neck laying his chest over Adam's body. His huge arm circled his neck clamping Adam's face next to Mark's.

"You could fight back, you know," Mark said with a huge grin. Adam tried to free his pinned wrist. He pushed with his free hand weakly but knew there was no point. He was pinned with a serious submission hold loosely clamped on his body. He knew how to fight and even considered himself strong and fast, but found himself wrapped in Mark's weight and masculine aroma and just wanted to be held there by him. It dawned on him sharply. These aren't his feelings. It was as though they were inserted into his head.

"Good conclusion," Mark said as though he heard the conclusion spoken out loud. "But how do you counter it? It's a pheromonal attack. You don't want to fight someone that you really get off on being dominated by. So what do you do?" Rolling to his side Mark hauled on Adam's wrist and surrounded Adam's torso with his huge thighs.

Adam was no stranger to fighting and had a seriously ripped torso, the envy of his division at PI. Regardless, he knew his body would not be able to hold back an assault by those legs. With a kick and twist of his torso, he moved his knee over Mark's blocking the crushing trap from closing around him. He rose on his feet getting ready to leap away from Mark's hold. Mark tightened his arm around Adam's neck pulling him back to his chest.

His face made contact with Mark's warm chest. He was getting ready to jump and took in a deep breath. It was like inhaling a solvent. His head spun and his cock grew painfully hard. Mark easily pulled him back into his embrace. Face to face, Adam felt Mark's legs encircle his torso slowly locking behind him. He couldn't even think of resisting. The initial pressure from the weight of his legs was tight and Adam flexed his abs to try to get ready to be crushed.

Adam's hips involuntarily bucked as waves of pleasure rolled through him. He had never felt anything so arousing. The texture of his own Boxer shorts was enough to make him writhe in ecstasy. Mark placed his hand over Adam's face. The smell of his skin was so intoxicating Adam began chewing on the meaty flesh of Mark's palm. He took in three deep breaths taking in more of Mark's aroma.

Squeezing his legs together, Mark tightened a crushing hold on Adam's waist. Unable to defend himself, Adam lost all the air from his lungs under the crushing pressure. His cock was so hard he ached. He tried to cum, but his body just wouldn't. He whimpered quietly, his hip bucking.

Mark let off the pressure and let Adam breathe. "Let's not lose the fun parts of the moment." Mark said. "I could've just killed you. In a moment, I'll show you what you need to do to resist the pheromone attack. But before that, is there something I can do for you? Perhaps relieve some deep need?"

Adam found himself pleading between breaths, "Please don't stop touching me! Please!" He felt Mark's hard cock pushing into his abdominals and rubbed himself over his cock. Mark moaned quietly. Adam locked his lips onto Mark's and kissed him deeply.

Coming up for breath he straddled Mark's chest, struggling to get his boxers off one leg at a time. Mark laughed as Adam tried to get himself free. Finally naked, he threw himself on Mark and kissed him again. He rubbed his cock up and down the ridges of Mark's abdominal ridgesl, amazed at the sleekness of his skin. He backed up and found Mark's cock pressed right against his ass.

He paused with a sudden claxon of fear. *He's going to fuck me. I will not get away from this without him fucking me.* Mark's face grew serious for a moment. "Oh no man, I am not a rapist. We'll go there when you ask real nice, like a friend. I know I have you in my control and you've wanted this quietly for a long time, but you have to ask..."

"Deal," Adam said breathlessly, not even fazed this time by the telepathic eavesdropping. "Have you ever done that? I mean with a Tredoran?"

Mark laughed. "Tredoran cocks are prehensile. They can seek your ass and take it while they hold you down. They can even shake your hand with it if they wanted..." Mark suddenly grinned and rolled Adam over onto his back, covering the smaller man with his muscular bulk, while holding most of his weight on his arms. He kissed Adam's neck and kissed his pectoral. He kissed his way down Adam's abs until the agent nearly screamed, his cock aching for release.

With gentle precision, he slipped his mouth over Adam's cock and swirled his tongue over and under his head. Still unable to cum, Adam arched his hips into the air. Mark felt his ass and reached his hands under the small of his back. "Nice," whispered Mark. "If I knew the Government was going to send me a beautiful man like you, I would've come home years ago. God Bless America." Mark slowly covered Adam with his body, slowly wrapping his huge muscular arms around him. Adam could smell that beautiful aroma and feel the warmth of his body. He was unable to see he was so horny.

"You can cum now. I'm here for you," Mark whispered is Adam's ear. All control gone, he howled like an animal and covered the two of them with four huge shots of cum. His hips bucked into Mark in spasms of pleasure. Struggling frantically, Adam's face met Mark's and locked lips. He kissed Mark deeply and passionately. Pulling the huge man on top of him, he wrapped his arm around Mark's neck like a drowning man, securing a deep kiss.

He heard the door open and his mind struggled to care. He knew that it was a serious problem for someone to just casually walk in. He saw Mark sit up and turn toward the kitchen. The shots filled the apartment with thunder. Two shots hit Mark in the neck and shoulder, spraying blood all over Adam.

Mark slumped forward on top of Adam. Struggling to extricate himself from Mark's last embrace, Adam looked to see staff Lieutenant Kirk holding the gun. He lowered it and walked out.

Adam was insane with rioting emotions. The soup of pheromones coursing through his mind fought with his PI training. He looked at Mark.

He was smiling. "Didn't hurt," he whispered. "Go get him. Use what I showed you." He held his hand over the bleeding wound at his neck. The whiteness of the bed was just amplifying the horror. "Go get him and stop his second attack."

Like a child comprehending math for the first time, Adam stood woodenly. "Kirk," he called out. He rounded the corner to see Kirk waiting by the door. He looked at Adam, standing blood-soaked and naked. Kirk had a sad look. Adam let out a breath and concentrated. Kirk gave a confused blink. Probably just like that Roller-coaster feeling he felt back at the terminal Adam guessed. Then he relaxed visibly. "Give me the gun," Adam said.

As though he never thought of doing anything else, he handed Adam the gun. He looked at the gun in his sticky blood soaked hand. He was amazed at the simplicity of the power and what little effort it took to use it.

He ran back to Mark's side and Kirk followed. He touched the call switch on the back of his head. Mark had lost a lot of blood and looked ashen. "This is Flint; code mercy! The Prodigal has been shot!"

Look for part II: Adam's trial

VOICE MAIL
CHAPTER ONE

August 12, 1988

SKRICK The machine made that noise again. Darrin hated voicemail and that sound it made before every message was even worse. Lucky there

were only fifteen messages this morning.

"Trent! I have your briefcase in my office. It's bad enough I had to chew you out for being drunk on company time..." Mr. Kaufman could never get the hang of the new system. But the system was installed five years ago, with no hope of the Old Man changing his habits. The system wasn't new anymore.

The Old Man gave Trent's mail address to Darrin. He usually does. Darrin knew Trent was always drinking, so this came as no surprise. He couldn't decide whether he should be concerned that all the boss' messages intended for him were being given to someone else or whether someone could drink constantly in this company and not visibly upset the operation. He decided last month that he didn't want to know.

Darrin Kraft had reached the point where he discovered that the job he always thought he wanted was shit, but it was comfortable shit, and he couldn't bring himself to change it. He had sawed the corners off the rest of his mind so he couldn't think about backing out of the position. Otherwise he'd have to recover those parts so he could remember how to compose resumes and look for employment without feeling like a corporate hooker.

Other than that, life was fine.

As he considered not considering his plight, the string of messages bled out of the dented voice box of the Message Master 4000. He looked at the dented and dusty equipment and remembered when the company got it. It was supposed to be the state of the art in office supply. Just then Darrin decided that he had to leave this place. His chest stopped hurting. He had to be right, he concluded.

"SKRITCK" The next message started. "Darrin, good to find your number. This is Alex Kasheski. I'll be in town this week. I'll be over to your place on Saturday and we'll wrestle. Prepare to lose, Dude!" There was that usual wicked chuckle Alex made when challenging a bud to wrestle.

Darrin paled as the machine ground to a halt. He fumbled his coffee onto the floor and pounded the stapler when he meant to slap the replay button on the machine. He played the message back and listened intently. "Prepare to lose..." was issued again with that chuckle.

He hadn't heard Alex's voice since college. His hands shook and he felt tears on his face. He stopped to check. He was sure that he didn't feel anything, but his eyes were leaking. His chest didn't hurt, so that had to be good, right? The big whopper starts like this, right? He knew that was how the big one comes, the big hammer in the chest.

But he wasn't having a heart attack. He just heard Alex's voice, that's all. His hands shook uncontrollably. After all these years; six years was it? All this time he was still afraid of wrestling Alex. This time was going to be worse.

The inescapable truth was that Alex died six years ago.

Darrin drove home a trembling wreck; he was mildly amazed to find himself in the driveway and not in a ditch. He walked straight to the bar in his house. He crossed the cream carpeting in the huge room with 30' ceilings. Pastel blue walls, a black leather sofa, all usually ignored. He spent more time in his room. The bar was covered in mail and dirty glasses. He was sure he wanted a drink, but if he was going to have to wrestle Alex tomorrow, he would need to be in better condition. Sure, OK, he had a day to get into better shape.

He took off his shirt, slowly unbuttoning it. He dropped it on the floor. Standing in front of the full length mirror covering the door to the bookcases in the living room, he looked at his body. He fought the middle-age spread daily with his workout. He flexed. He wasn't ripped like he was in the old days, but he had more mass and the shadow of his six pack lingered. But time gave him a strange view. His chest was large and thick with muscle. He considered it the base of his favorite hold, his bearhug.

But that was long ago. The guys in the office would die in that embrace and it wasn't cool to even mention that.

He dropped and quickly drove through fifty push-ups. He remembered when he and Alex tried to outdo each other. Alex was always stronger.

Except when it counted.

They said Alex's appendix burst and he died in his bed, alone and in pain. But Darrin knew Alex died because he couldn't say uncle.

He remembered Alex's face, beet red, trapped in Darrin's crushing bodyscissors, too tired to fight back any more. He finally got Alex back for all those nasty body scissors His best friend used to trap him in.

He squeezed Alex for a long time. He slipped his bare thighs around Alex's shirtless six-packed torso and squeezed. Mounted on his back Darrin watched as Alex just withstood the punishment, slowly crumpling into the mat. Eager to hear Alex say he surrendered, he knew it was coming soon; the struggles and stopped, Darrin dug his knees deeper into Alex's sides.

His handsome face twisted into a scream, no sound, just his muscular body in a trembling exertion. Darrin felt the heat from his body, sweat pouring off him. His surrender was obvious. His breathing nearly stopped and he stopped fighting. It was weird. He just quit, but never said he gave up or surrendered.

If Darrin were more a dick at wrestling, he would've felt justified in crushing the crap out of him until he verbalized he quit. But he couldn't. He let Alex go and Alex just lay there, limply.

"You okay?"

"I don't feel so good," was all Alex said. Darrin helped him get to the locker room at the gym and went home. He never had to help Alex up before. The next day the news was out. Alex was dead. It didn't matter what everyone said. Darrin knew Alex was dead because of him.

Darrin fumbled with his car keys. He probably needed to get back to the office. He was sure he needed to go to lunch, feeling so pained and lousy, regardless what the management said about lunches on Saturday being cancelled. He fished his shirt off the floor and slid it over his shoulders.

"My aren't we full of our selves today?" A voice right behind him said. Darrin whirled to see Alex standing there, his Eagles t-shirt, the one he used to work

out in, still on his torso. He still had it. Darrin dropped his keys and stammered.

"No problem, dude," Alex said whisking the keys off the floor. "I'll drive. You look like shit anyway."

"You...you can't drive my car." Darrin stammered.

"It's not broken again, is it?" Alex said turning on his heel facing Darrin.

"No...you're..." Darrin couldn't say it.

"Dead?" Alex turned and looked at himself in the mirror that covered the bookcases. "So what? I look *real* good." He adjusted his collar like he was dressed real well. He was right too. He didn't look a day older than he did in college, top of his form. He even exuded that glowing muscular warmth he always had.

He opened the door and walked outside leaving Darrin to decide whether he should stay and let his dead friend drive his car away or if he should follow. It only took a split second for Darrin to be right on the dead man's heels.

"I'm sure you're wondering..." Alex said as Darrin caught up.

"Why you're here?" Darrin finished his sentence.

"You already know why I'm here; to show you how to get out of that cage. You just open the door and, vi-o-la!"

"Voila, you mean..."

"That French shit again... whatever," Alex said as he unlocked Darrin's decaying Fiero. "I'm sure you're wondering where we're going to wrestle. I figure point Park will do."

"Can't. There's too many police there these days," Darrin said.

"Okay, I'll drive to Altoona if we have to. We'll find something."

Darrin opened the passenger door. It wouldn't lock any more anyway. He scraped the bills and mail off the seat and threw himself in. Alex jammed the car into drive. Darrin just stared forward. He couldn't look at Alex.

"Jeez, they call me dead," Alex said after five minutes of the silence. He turned on the radio to wDVE. "Shit, the music sucks anymore."

"DVEs still cool," Darrin defended his favorite station.

"No, all the music sucks now. Doesn't anyone know how to use a guitar any more?" Alex messed with the rear view mirror and it came off in his hand. "Shit! well, I guess we have to live a little dangerously, huh? Don't look back. Can't!"

Darrin was still staring forward. "Why are you doing this to me?"

"What?"

"Alex," Darrin said through his teeth. "You're dead. Why are you here?"

"Because I love you," Alex said. He let go of the wheel and slapped a kiss on Darrin's lips. Darrin struggled to grab the wheel and break out of the kiss at the same time. He almost immediately regretted it. Alex was warm and he tasted so good. A wave of incredible desire surged over him. He was hard in an instant.

He pushed Alex away, "I can't ...can't do this!"

"You don't have to. I told you I'd drive..."

"This! I can't wrestle you!" Darrin was nearing frantic.

Alex let out a deep sigh. "What did you say? You summon me from the dead and can't follow through with the simplest part of your end of the deal? Do you think I'm going away?"

"Fuck that man! I didn't summon you!" Darrin was pissed. "I don't want this!"

"Oh, so you jerkin' your pud thinking of how we used to paste our bodies together with sweat, pokin each other with our hard cocks, and wishing as hard as you can that we could do it again," his hot breath was in Darrin's ear. Darrin tried to ignore the obvious driving danger. "You were pledging your love to me. Dude! I get a woodie thinking about it. Here checkitout!." Alex pulled open his shorts. Darrin just looked away. "You wished for me. I'm here!"

"It doesn't work that way," Darrin pleaded. Alex was right. He wished for his death to just go away.

"Daaaarin. Come to reality. I'll serve coffee. Yes, it does work that way," he chuckled. "You see, that night you wished, your semen splattered on a rock in your back yard that was..."

"I don't want to hear this!!"

"...part of an altar that was used in a uncompleted ritual of fertility seven hundred years ago on the marriage of a daughter in an old tribe you won't even understand and the wishing never was consummated."

"Shut up!" Darrin shouted.

"Make me!" Alex entered the freeway from an exit ramp making Darrin just scream. "Jeez! You are so touchy!" He threw the car into a spin and gunned the car in the opposite direction so the car was driving southbound.

"Stop the car! I want out!" Darrin shouted.

"That's right! You want out! Ever since you got that job, you've been so content that you don't have to make any more decisions of substance. You've figured out where you're going to work, but that sucks! You figured out where you live, but you never see it, why? See previous gripe for answer! You're always working! You figured out who you're going to fuck but Diane left you because you were still hung up over fucking me and lamenting my death; you are pathetic!"

Darrin placed his hands over his ears. "You are not real. You are exhaustion and vodka talking."

Alex ignored him and continued louder. "All the life decisions have been made by you or for you and now you're done! Just cruise from here!" Alex pointed his finger at Darrin while he cringed against the door of the car. "All that you left yourself in the decision department, man, is cappuccino or latte! And you wonder why you're depressed? You fucked up! And Darrin, buddy, the most pathetic part is that you've stopped because you're terrified of being wrong; no decisions, no fault!"

Alex slammed on the brakes and the car spun wildly. It landed in the median facing north. Alex jumped out of the car and started walking south. Darrin opened the door and stood. Alex stripped off his shirt and his body shone in the noonday sun like gold.

"You're pathetic. Darrin!" Alex said, turning and walking toward him, arms outspread. "You are so damn selfish I want to beat the crap out of you!"

"Selfish?!" Darrin snapped. His voice reached a screeching tone. "I have given everything to my company, my wife, the IRS, everyone," Darrin whined. "How am I selfish?!"

"Because you wished for me to come and you won't have the decency to wrestle me or even be able to put up a fight!" Alex said. Darrin was stunned. Alex looked frantic about that point. "Do you think I can go back until this is done? Nope! Wrong again, asshole!"

Darrin just trembled. It sunk in how real this was. "I'm sorry," he said.

"Yes, you are!" Alex said, furiously. He slumped on the rear hood of the car and buried his face in his hands.

"What can I do?" Darrin asked.

Alex took a deep breath. "Come here," He punctuated the command with a gentle beckoning hand. Darrin walked up to him and Alex put his arm around him. "You need to wrestle me and beat me."

"I can't," Darrin said flatly.

"I know," Alex said with gentle patience in his voice. Gently rubbing Darrin's chest, his warm breath in the ear as he held him quietly close, Alex comforted Darrin. Darrin wanted to just sink into that hold and keep him there forever. Tears leaked down his cheek again. "So I'll come back and try this again." He let out a deep sigh and covered his face again.

"You okay?" Darrin asked.

"No, Darrin," he said with deep exasperation. "I'm dead."

"Oh," Darrin said.

Alex uncovered his face and Darrin saw how this was wearing on him. Dark circles were suddenly under his eyes. "And I'm so tired." "Your eyes," Darrin said. "You look so..."

"My friend, I understand this is all very new to you," Alex said. "It is to me too. It takes a lot of energy to live up to your expectations. You go find a trainer and muscle up. I'm coming for you in a month. You better beat me or I'll thrash your middle-aging ass." The intensity of the comment was betrayed by his rakish smile.

"Okay," Darrin said.

Alex grabbed his shirt off the ground and walked south. "You gonna need that?" Darrin asked.

"I'm cold man," Alex said. "You can warm me up later." Alex walked about a hundred yards and faded away into misty indistinction, like fog under the intensity of the sunrise. Darrin stared at the strangely deserted noontime highway.

CHAPTER TWO

"You don't seem to understand," Darrin said. "Three afternoons a week I'm taking some personal time." Mr Kaufmann was not even close to understanding.

"You need time, take it," Kaufmann said in his usual grandfatherly tone. "Did you have a plan for making this time up?"

"Making it up? I'm already working nearly double-overtime in unscheduled hours,' Darrin said for the third time. "I think six hours a week is not such a big deal, since I'm here every day of the week."

"Well, Darrin, you know you have duties and we all depend on you," Kaufmann stammered.

"I have Johnson and Shirly Kelso trained. She's really a big asset," Darrin said for the third time.

"She's good at making coffee, but handling major securities?"

"She finished her MBA in finance at Penn State, paid by the company. This is what she was hired to do," Darrin suggested. He knew she was hired for appearances and she was beginning to suspect this herself. The Nintendo N64 game system in the cubicle was the first hint. It was the most up-to-date electronic system in the building.

Kaufmann did what he did when he had to make a big decision. He called his secretary. "Jennifer?" He said into his intercom. "I need to see the master schedule."

"I will show you this schedule, sir, but you may not hold a pen while reading it!" The voice of order flatly came back over the intercom.

"I promise," he said like a first grader. Jennifer came in. As always, dressed to lethal perfection, down to the nails. She was a woman of direct African heritage, Nigerian, such a double plus, Kaufmann had to have her as his personal secretary. The schedule was laid before Kaufmann and folded out...all five sections of it.

"Oh, I see," Kaufmann said like he always did when he didn't see at all.

Taking her cue, Jennifer pointed, "These are Darrin's hours."

"Well, it says here you're only scheduled for 40 hours like everyone else. I'm not sure why we're having this conversation." Darrin wanted to cry.

He left Kauffmann's office with his six hours after promising to make them up over various holidays. He didn't care. He was going to work those Holidays anyway. He would've agreed to anything as long as he didn't have to tell Kaufmann that he was training to beat his dead friend in a wrestling match. He was sure the boss thought he was getting regular visits to a shrink or something. It was an option he considered but chose the gym instead.

Brik Manson was finishing up the paperwork verifying the

general health of each of his training clients. It was his cover-your-ass policy to make sure no one sued him, or if they had to waste their time in such a fashion, they'd lose.

These days, he was able to do the paperwork for his alter ego Brik Manson without giggling or laughing a gruff noise of disgust. He really didn't get as many clients able to pay when he went with him real name Francis Klinken. When he said that name, he couldn't shake the image of something unsavory stuck to his privates as a result of bad hygiene. Francis Klinken. Ick!

He looked nothing like a Klinken, or what he thought a Klinken might look like. He had blond hair and solid flaring shoulders that rolled to a narrow wasp waist, braided from cables of muscle. Charming smile. glasses (no contacts, he hated the phoniness) and an nice all over tan.

In College he got the name Brik. He played Lacrosse for some time and some football. His reputation was solid; he was solid. Brik worked. Nothing goes through. Must go over. Brik.

And Manson was a scary word.

When he got his fourth black belt in martial arts, he took the new name. He figured if he made a name imposing enough, he wouldn't have to speak gruffly with anyone ever.

He watched Darrin come into the gym. The picture of his teacher, Larry Wise, a big man that fought like madness itself and taught like a loving brother, sat in the corner. Brik looked at the picture, a private ritual. He remembered asking Larry the same question he was about to hear.

Brik got out his standard waiver for the mentally challenged, chuckling, wondering if Larry would've done the same for him. He usually didn't have a client sign one of these, but he knew what was coming. He thought he'd seen this one a million times. Brik was wrong.

"May I speak to someone about signing up with a personal trainer," Darrin asked Brik.

"Sign here," Brik said in a resonant deep voice.

"I just want to talk to someone," Darrin objected.

"No," Brik said with a smile. "You want to muscle up so you can beat someone in a fight."

"How did you know that?" Darrin asked defensively. He was just a little sick of being so obvious to the world that people could just tell what he was thinking.

"I know that because I am good," Brik said with an even bigger smile. "Who's the guy you have to fight and why?"

"He's an old friend from college," Darrin said quietly as he read over the waiver. "Why is there a clause about me not claiming you put me up to a fight?"

"People are stupid," he said. "Don't be stupid and everything will be fine."

"Okay," Darrin said as he signed. "I won't be." He worried immediately. He really wasn't sure if he could work an hour a day with anyone and not be stupid. He suddenly hated his boss and his job.

"What sort of fight do you need to win," Brik asked. "Street, legit boxing, Martial art, wrestling, No-Holds-Barred?"

"He said he's coming to kick my ass in a month," Darrin said.

"Now you know everything I do."

"Don't make that mistake. I know way more than you do." Brik said without looking up from the paperwork. "Is he likely to kill you?"

"No," Darrin said. "In fact he needs me alive."

"Okay, let's get started with some grappling and see what's needed after that," he still smiled. Darrin hated that. He knew this man was going to grind him into the mat a hundred times. Then he looked around.

Darrin shifted his attention to the facilities. Like a great big warehouse, the place was huge, with sections of the floor separated by tall temporary walls. It gently reminded him of the cubicles at work, but more spacious.

"Why the temp walls?"

"We pull this whole space apart and have monthly matches here with seating. I can move the whole thing out of here. Have a big match, and have the whole thing set back up for the morning work out crew. With your gold membership here, the fights are free to attend with a guaranteed audition for fights if you want to compete."

He looked over Darrin and said, "It looks like your training schedule's gonna be a full one. When did you last do any sports?"

"I wrestled in College," Darrin said looking at the weight rooms in front.

"You any good?" Brik asked.

"I was one of the best," Darrin said absently.

With that Brik swept his left leg out from under him, pushed his shoulder and watched Darrin fall flat on the mat.

In two strides he walked over and straddled Darrin surrounding his torso with his huge legs. He slapped his meaty hand over Darrin's throat and squeezed, gently and in the right place. There was no air moving through his windpipe at all. The warm fire of Brik's muscular thighs held him tightly, but it was comfortable. The hard muscle seemed too huge. Unable to believe he was here already, Darrin squirmed and found he wasn't moving anywhere. Darrin knew Brik was being nice.

"You are not one of the best any more," Brik said in a kind, quiet fatherly tone. "When I tell you something about your form, please assume I am correct. If you doubt me or argue with me, expect an object lesson like this one. These days you suck as a fighter and walk like an ox. You need to learn how to move again and dump some bad habits."

Brik let Darrin's throat loose but his hand barely shifted position, staying just a flex away from strangling his client. "Yes, sir," Darrin said with his first breath. He knew he had to get better and confidence in Brik was strangely easy. At no point did Brik threaten.

"Good answer. First, no more alcohol, No tobacco and cut processed sugar. Soda is gone. If I ever see you drink a soda, expect me to terminate our contract and you will be charged the early termination fee."

"No more...?"

"No more soda," Brik said with authority, quietly. "Do you want to win?"

"Yes," Darrin said, swallowing his argument. "Sir."

"Good," Brik's massive thighs pressed into Darrin's soft ribcage. "You will not drink any more soda. You will motivate yourself with your will or I will motivate you with fear. I prefer you to motivate yourself. Know this up front."

It went on like that for about five minutes with Brik on Darrin's chest, held firmly in place while he received orders from his trainer. He finished with, "And I really don't want to know the identity of the guy you're going to fight. I will not be a witness in any illegal proceedings willingly. Do we understand each other?"

"Yes sir!"

"Know one more thing," Brik said, waiting for Darrin's response. "I am not like other trainers. If you don't like my style, you may leave at any time you say you're done. Prepare to be treated like my son. Expect me to raise you like you knew nothing. Expect me to love you like you were part of me."

Darrin stammered, "Sir...?"

"Don't be an ass," Brik said derisively. "You are not required to reciprocate. It would not be love if you had to give me something back. That would be blackmail. Understand you will see me concerned in parts of your life that you think are private. All secrets you think you have are, as of now, my business. I am required to hold them in confidence, but you are required to divulge. I will know you. I will touch you. Every place on your body is mine to touch." He punctuated this by dismounting Darrin like a horse and slapping his other hand over Darrin's crotch.

Without causing pain, he squeezed Darrin's nuts in his huge hand. "No...sir no. Please." Darrin squirmed.

"Shut up," Brik said very softly. Darrin took two deep breaths to pin down his panic. He was breathing normally in about a minute. "Very good. You pass the first test. If you like this, cool. If you don't, you will learn to stop me and know when it's about to happen. If I don't have your whole body to train, you will learn incomplete garbage. We don't have much time, so make this count."

He paused in thought and then asked in a quieter tone. "What do you do for a living?"

"I work with Kaufmann and Smith as an investment..." He was abruptly cut off.

"It's killing you. Arrange for some substantial time off. Two days a week should be yours to enjoy," Brik ordered.

"But, I'll be fired. They don't tolerate..."

"Neither do I. I give orders," Brik said. "Besides, your first fight is in two weeks. You'll be in the octagon with one of my other students."

Darrin felt the creeping panic set in and his face was wet. He rubbed his face and felt tears. Just like when he heard Alex's voice on the voicemail com.

"Yes sir," Darrin said. His voice was visibly changed. Brik hoped it was something more like resolve and not resignation. "Now get up and I want to see you run a mile. That's four times around the perimeter of this facility. You have ten minutes. Get to it."

Darrin scrambled to his feet and started on his run. He ran in a couple different directions before he got the idea of where he was going. He discarded parts of his suit as he ran.

He didn't notice Johnson as he ran past him in front of the building. Johnson just stared. He pulled his beeping phone out of his pocket. "Johnson here."

"So where is he?" Kaufmann asked.

Johnson lied. "Um...he's shopping for ... home furnishings. Looks like he's going to do some remodeling. It's not like we thought. No one's courting him with another job offer."

"I'm not buying it. You find out what he's dong. Did he see you?"
"No, he doesn't look around much," Johnson said. "Good work, Johnson, keep at it."

A Boner Book

CHAPTER THREE

Darrin walked into the gym looking like hell. His eye and cheek were swollen and looking weepy. He knew he had lots of work to do.

"Is Brik here?" he asked the woman at the desk. She dialed the back room extension with a look of grave concern. Brik came up and just swore. "Jezzees...you dumb shit! I got it Sue," he said to the clerk. She had a cold pack ready like this was a habit. She pressed it against Darrin's head and stepped back as they walked slowly back to the mat room.

"He was all over me," Darrin said.

"Well, I suppose you're done with this crazy notion now. I know I was rough on you but you need to take some appreciation for the gains you've made and keep them. Make more. Do it slowly."

"He's coming back next month," Darrin said.

Brik made a twisted face. His whole muscular frame tensed up and with a deep breath, he relaxed. "You need authorities in this one, man." He was not amused. "This man is clearly stalking you."

"Haunting is more correct," Darrin said to his shoes.

"Whatever," Brik said.

"That won't work," Darrin said. "And I know you're about to tell me this is a typical thing a battered man says and that it's all better if no one else were involved. This man can not be detained."

"He a diplomat or something?" Brik asked.

"No," Darrin said. "He's..."

The question was answered by a voice behind them. "Now that would be against the rules, Darrin," Alex said coming around the wall. He looked fabulous. Darrin's heart hammered in his chest. Even when he makes a surprise entrance, he looks hotter than he ever did.

Darrin stood looking at his dead friend with some fear and love at the same time. He walked over to Alex. "Are you alright ... besides that, I mean. "

"I'm fine, man." he said with a smile. "I'm here to see if I can get this going faster."

"I don't know man." Darrin said. Brik was just standing by watching this exchange.

"So this is the man you gotta beat?" He couldn't keep the incredulous rudeness out of his voice. "He's a kid."

"Watch your mouth," Alex said. "I'm here to see if our guy is okay."

"After you beat the crap out of him?" Brik was steamed. "You better leave. This place is for members only."

"I know that. I don't care," Alex said laughing. Darrin slapped his forehead, burying his face in his hands.

"Don't worry," Brik said walking closer to Alex. "I just have to say that before I slap someone...keeps it legal."

"You gonna challenge me?" Alex asked walking up to the stud. "You know, that might be fun."

Brik pushed Alex in the chest, a shove that would send smaller opponents sprawling. He could feel the muscle in Alex's chest flex. It was like stone. As Alex stood his ground, he smiled. It was a warm and friendly smile. Brik couldn't believe the enjoyment this kid got from challenging him.

"My turn," Alex shoved Brik in the chest and sent him sprawling on the floor, skidding 20 feet. Alex walked over to him. "You slip or something?"

Brik was very fast and took advantage of his lower position. His muscular shoulder hit Alex in the abs as he launched himself in a tackle. Alex dropped back and rolled. They tumbled over several times from the momentum of Brik's massive legs.

Alex nearly straddled Brik. There was a small momentum left to their tumble that Brik used to settle Alex onto his back. Alex's legs slipped around Brik's torso and locked behind him. Alex's legs began to squeeze Brik's ripped torso. Lost in the enfolding golden muscle, Brik's waist was squeezed by Alex's tightly grasping legs. Brik tightened up his abs to resist the squeeze and get to the grapple.

Trying for a hold on Brik's wrist, Alex grabbed at the bigger man. Brik twisted his wrist out of Alex's grasp and slipped his forearm under Alex's chin. Another inch and it would be a fine forearm choke.

Like he was jointless, Alex twisted to the right, forcing Brik's elbow to the mat. His squeezing hold slipped open and lifted Brik's left leg. In a circular sprawl, Brik was lifted off Alex's torso and flipped with Alex shortly following. Brik rolled and disengaged.

Both men were in their wrestler's crouch three feet from each other. Alex sprung on Brik, a hasty move, but effective. Brik fell off balance and rolled. Alex landed on his torso, straddling Brik. He fired a fist into Brik's face that didn't do much damage, but served to enrage the trainer.

Brik lifted Alex off his body to throw him and found Alex slip through his arms onto his throat. He spun toward the mat to guard himself, dragging Alex's arm over. Side by side, both wrestlers shoved each other, Alex trying to free his arm, Brik trying to keep the kid off his neck.

Alex's arm slipped out of the hold but timed so Brik could slide his grasp down to Alex's neck. Fumbling for a grip, Brik's hand closed on Alex's throat. He squeezed and Alex made a choking sound close to laughter. Brik squeezed harder.

Like lightning, he released the grip and stood. He bolted ten feet from Alex and whirled to stare at him. Alex laughed. He slapped the mat and rolled in hysterical laughter.

"That's not funny," Darrin said.

"He found out our little...secret," Alex said between gales of laughter.

"Did you know," Brik said with a tremble. "Your bad mannered friend has no pulse."

Alex just howled with laughter. "Hey man, I lost it somewhere. Can you help me find it?"

108

"Stop it," Darrin said. "No sir, he doesn't."

"Fuck this, man," Brik said. "This was not in the deal."

"I know, but I need you to..."

"You need a shrink... and you!" He said raging at Alex. You need...

"A decent burial?" Alex was only smiling this time. "could it possibly occur to you that's what you're helping us with?"

"So he has to beat you?" Brik said ,letting this all sink in. "Or you won't go away?"

"Right!" Alex said with glee. "Man, he got that much faster than you did."

"Shut up," Darrin said.

"No way," Brik said. "I want my termination fee." he said to Darrin and turned to walk. Brik suddenly remembered Larry and wanted to swear. He told Darrin this was love. He was blinded by his private war of honor just enough to miss Alex. In a flash, he found himself wrapped in the strongest body lock he ever felt.

Alex wrapped his arms around Brik's head and his thick legs surrounded Brik's waist. The squeeze was incredible. Brik sunk to his knees from the pain.

"You will teach this sorry son of a bitch how to beat me, or I can't go back," Alex doubled his squeeze and Brik let out a strangled groan. Alex's arm had Brik's throat circled in a powerful rear choke. All Brik could think was what a fool he was to let such a kindergarten hold sink in. Brik had never felt a grip so strong or so desperate. He threw two quick elbows at Alex to try to dislodge him. Alex hung on.

The pressure on Brik's ripped torso tightened and tightened. "I can go much tighter, wanna see?" Alex said into Brik's ear. The squeeze intensified little by little, Brik shook as he flexed to hold off the assault on his torso.

"I didn't ask to come here. It was an accident that Darrin wished me here. He was lonely. You can understand that, I hope." Mark said. There was a note of grief in his voice that Darrin could tell. "If you won't teach him, I'll send you to God to explain all this."

Brik tried to fight, squirming and thrashing violently, landing random punches, but the hold on his solid body dug in deeper. Alex let nothing up in his squeeze. Darrin just watched in awe as Brik's waist was constricted so tightly by the powerful legs surrounding him that his already narrow waist looked like it was squeezed into an unbelievably small space. He was amazed that such a hold could ever happen from someone Alex's size.

"Train him," Alex said, and loosened his hold to get an answer from Brik.

"I will not be blackmailed," Brik hissed. "AAAaaagggh!!" He screamed as Alex squeezed him to punish the response.

"Train him!!" Alex ordered the trainer. Brik just shook his head negative.

"Alex, "Darrin said. "Stop this..."

"Stay out of this asshole," Alex said viciously. "You've caused enough trouble. Don't help."

Darrin responded by kicking Alex in the jaw and snapping his head backwards. "I said let go!!"

Seeing help from Darrin, Brik struggled harder in the suffocating embrace. Alex shook his head and smiled, "Hey Brik, our boy has balls!"

Brik was sure sanity had taken lunch for the day. "I will not be blackmailed..." he managed through the chokehold and squeeze combination.

"I'll cut you in half," Alex threatened and squeezed Brik harder than he had endured so far. Darrin looked at the pressure on Brik's torso and couldn't believe a man could be crushed like that and still be conscious. Darrin heard a loud pop and Brik groaned in pain. Alex's muscular thighs pressed deeply into Brik's torso, striating as he constricted relentlessly. Brik's face was red and he couldn't respond. His eyes fluttered and he looked glassy.

Alex loosened up on the trainer, "Train him. You have no choice."

"I...will...not...be...black..." He didn't have to finish the statement.

"You kill him, we're no better off." Darrin said. "He has to be convinced, not tortured."

"You said you loved him," Alex said. He was really concerned now. He had no plan for Brik refusing. "You said you loved him. Make him beat me! Please!"

He let go of the big trainer. He snapped to his feet and seemed to be transparent. The sunny warm glow his skin that radiated when he was happy was gone.

Brik gasped and held his stomach while he drank in breath as fast as he could breathe, his face pressed into the mat. Tears leaked from the side of one eye. Darrin slowly walked over to him and touched him.

"Fuck off," Brik said. The tears were more apparent. Darrin held him, unphased by the rebuff. He touched Brik's stomach and held his head against his chest. Heaving breaths, Brik cried. "Shit... fuck... shit..." he kept saying. Warring with the urge to cry and breathe and soaring with the adrenaline and endorphin of a good hard squeeze, Brik tried to gather his composure. The dead guy was real and really hurt him. He was really right and he promised to love Darrin.

Alex bent to his knee and wiped a tear from Brik's face. "I'm sorry," Alex sounded flat and monotone, but the mere touch from Alex made Brik's emotions race out of control. Brik looked into his gray face and saw Alex's real pain. He realized this was the aura of an restless dead man, grieving without the ability to express anything unless someone living cared.

Reeling in Alex's inexpressible grief, Brik sobbed in Darrin's arms and stopped fighting the waves of emotion that he felt for Alex. This was all against the rules. He was never emotional in front of a client. All the rules were broken. Dammit!

Woodenly, Alex fell into their mutual embrace. Brik took two deep breaths and his returning strength was apparent, suddenly. "I'm sorry, Alex. I was...selfish."

"Thank...you," Alex said with a voice distant like an echo. "This has...to ...end...please."

"We'll make it end," Brik said.

"I'm ... so...cold," Alex said. "Hold me, please."

"Okay," he said quietly. "How much time."

"We said a month, but I really need this to go as fast as you can."

"Why?" Darrin asked. "You said I have a month."

"There's things going on that I didn't know about before," Alex said.

"What thing?" Brik asked.

"I am becoming less and less human. I'm afraid I may not be able to play my role in this... I'm so cold..."

"Becoming less human?" Darrin mulled over the concept. "What are you becoming?"

"You wouldn't like it. Keep me warm... please..." like a sand castle crumbling in the surf, Alex became indistinct and fell apart in their embrace, evaporating as he dissolved. Just a warm musky smell was left as they both realized Alex was gone.

CHAPTER FOUR

September 10, 1988

Alex was expected in another week. Darrin was amazed at the appearance he had in the mirror. His six-pack was back and he had more energy than he had had in five years.

"One Hundred Push-ups!" Brik had entered.

Darrin hit the mat and pumped out push-ups in rapid succession. He finished the hundred and Brik clicked his stopwatch. "Five minutes and thirty-three seconds. Better. You've been practicing. Brik moved to a leg sweep and Darrin dodged. He drove for a takedown, immediately forcing Brik to sprawl and counter. Brik quickly turned and rolled Darrin over his hip onto the mat. Brik landed hard on Darrin's chest. Quickly, Darrin was fighting an elbow lock.

"You're done. Tap," It wasn't a suggestion. Darrin waited a couple seconds trying to escape and felt the connective tissues of his elbow and wrist separating. He tapped Brik's back frantically.

"What's the lesson?" Brik asked helping Darrin off the mat.

"Move to guard or half-guard when tossed. Keep arms in tighter.

Uh...and know when my arm's about to come apart." Darrin said. He was serious. The public match was in a couple hours. He was going up against Everett Mahan, another new guy. Mahan was ten years younger than Darrin.

Brik dove for surprise tackle and caught Darrin in the solar plexus with his shoulder. They went down hard with Brik on top. Darrin slid to his back andwrapped his arms around Brik's head. He pulled down and wrapped his legs around Birk's torso. Snapping his legs tight, he began looking for leverage on Brik's arms. The heat of his solid torso between his legs was overwhelming. Brik's hot breath on his chest smelled musky and drove Darrin to wanting his teacher badly. Even though he was reminded to keep him focus, his cock snapped hard.

"Ok, time for an advanced technique," Brik said. "I can see you like this position a whole lot. What about now?" He flexed his abs right over Darrin's swollen cock. Darrin moaned softly. Brik rocked forward and back a few times raking his cobblestone abs over Darrin's cock. Darrin's eyes rolled back and he felt a hot rush coming to his groin. Fighting embarrassment and distraction, Darrin tried to break the hold, but Brik pushed with his legs, wedging his torso between Darrin's thighs.

Darrin re-gripped his legs around Brik, fighting to control his teacher. Still driving with his legs, Darrin was forced into the cramped corner of the mat room, making the controlling nature of the guard less and less effective. His forward motion was still rubbing against Darrin's crotch, and Darrin knew he was close to cumming. With several well-placed pelvic thrusts, Brik drove Darrin to climax.

Darrin whimpered and then screamed as a torrent of hot cum filled his jock and soaked through to the grey t-shirt of his instructor. Brik just sat there grinning. "Now, you know how many evil locks and counters I can do from this position?" Brik asked.

"No," Darrin said panting. "I don't know what you know."

"Good you're learning," Brik said. "Don't be embarrassed. I like making guys cum." Darrin lifted his head off the mat to stare at Brik in shock. "Big deal, so do you." Brik said to the look. "Some of your opponents will be freaked by an erection and try to pull back. Some will see it as an advantage."

"It sure does make losing more pleasant," Darrin said. Brik stood and helped Darrin off the mat.

"So the guy you have to fight, he likes making you cum. You'll have to deal with that. It's probably the center of your conflict with each other." Brik stated.

Darrin was getting used to having Brik read his life like a book. This stung though. He knew this was the whole point of the fight with Alex. He had to get Alex to submit and get off this sex/love question of him. Darrin nodded. "Thank you, sir."

Brik stopped, "For what?" He looked levelly at Darrin.

"Thank you for helping me be a man," Darrin said.

Brik shook his head. "You are such a dork. This is fighting, not romance." Brik toweled off and walked to his office. Darrin really wanted to stop being such a dork, but he knew the emotions he had kept him training.

Mahan and his corner man walked in the front door past the line of guys lining up to buy a ticket for the fight. Darrin waved hi to him. Mahan just looked at him levelly like he was insane and moved to the locker room. Darrin shook his head and knew he was being a dork again. Mahan looked good. Short brush-cut blond hair. Broad shoulders and hard waist. He was nice. He watched Mahan walk away and missed Johnson paying for his seat.

Darrin looked out of the locker room at the lit and raised octagon. The four sets of bleachers filled quickly. The school showed great fights and the local neighborhood loved it. Brik kept the drugs and bookies mostly off premises and the place was clean. Even Public Television came.

Through a murmur he couldn't understand he finally heard his name. Right up to that point, he wasn't nervous. He'd been in wrestling matches in College. That was tense, but he was usually sure that no one would get broken. This was different.

Deep breath. *Look at you*, he said to himself. *Still afraid of this? Get down there!* He slowly walked down the aisle between the bleachers. The crowd had no idea who he was and didn't care. They roared.

Brik put the gloves on Darrin. "You know what to do. Look at me" He put his face right in Darrin's as he laced the gloves. There was no one else in reality, just Brik. He could feel Brik's massive chest pressed against his. That made everything good suddenly. "Tell your dick to calm down! Listen to me! I'm in your corner and I can see things you can't. If I tell you to do something, you do it! No thinking, do it! And Darrin! If you win, you get to go home with me tonight! Go win!" Darrin gawked at his instructor. Brik pushed him to the gate.

Darrin's head spun with the deep attraction he was feeling for his instructor.

Everett Mahan was called down the aisle. He didn't walk rather he stalked. Flat feet stomped down the aisle. *He's more scared than I am. Great.* As if he heard Darrin's thoughts, he met Darrin's eyes. Instant stare down. Mahan broke first, nervously. *I should win this.*

118

Johnson watched and laughed. He couldn't believe what he was seeing. It was good enough seeing an event on company time – hell, a spelling bee on company time would be a big gift. He couldn't believe that Darrin was going to do this. And this is what he went to the line with the boss over? I think the boss better worry about getting beaten up more than losing Darrin.

But he knew he could use this to his advantage. He rehearsed in his mind, "Well Mr. Kauffman, he's fighting at a local martial arts gym and he's practicing to kick your ass. Can I have his job?" Johnson laughed at his little joke.

He paid no attention to the kid that sat next to him. "Want some popcorn?" Alex asked Johnson as he sat. Alex had an extra bag and handed it to Johnson, who just stared at the unexpected friendliness. He took the bag, "Thanks."

"No problem, I brought an extra," Alex smiled and watched.

Darrin looked up into the crowd. He saw Johnson and Alex sitting next to each other. Alex waved. He nearly wet himself. "Oh shit."

"Look at your opponent!" Brik yelled. "Do *not* look into the crowd again or I'll kick your ass!" Darrin's head snapped back in time for the bell. Darrin looked at Everett Mahan. He pounded his gloved hands together and jogged in place. Wound like a spring, he was probably going to shoot for a takedown immediately.

The Bell. Here comes Mahan. He shot for a double leg takedown. Darrin was heavier and harder to move. He slapped his right on the back of Mahan's neck and pushed him to the mat. Slipping in traction, Mahan fell on his face. Closing a front face lock, he hoisted Mahan up trying to unbalance him.

Fast as a striking snake, Mahan's legs shot forward around Darrin's right leg. He slipped right out of Darrin's face lock and spun to the right as hard as he could. Darrin's right knee buckled. Darrin completed the spin and landed on his back scissoring Mahan's left leg in a half guard.

The crowd went wild. The first takedown usually does that. "Block your face! Arms tighter!" Brik yelled from his corner. Falling forward Mahan aimed a right rook to Darrin's face. "I said block!! Hold his head closer to your chest!" Darrin sucked at fists and took two more elbow shots to the head trying to block. He grabbed Mahan's right wrist while Mahan tried freeing his leg out of Darrin's guard.

They struggled for superiority for a solid minute. "Hey stud, you're doing really well!" It was Alex, just on the outside of the octagon. "Oh man, feel the muscle on this guy...jeez, how lucky to be you." Darrin hazarded a look to where he heard Alex. Standing right there next to Mahan's corner people. He wore his Eagles T-shirt and had that youthful glow. He could feel the warmth emanating from him. *He's so beautiful, for a dead guy.* Darrin felt his cock grow, even with his opponent on top of him swinging at his face.

Darrin landed a solid left hook in Mahan's face just as Mahan slipped out of the scissor guard on his leg. He spun a half turn and sat on Darrin's leg, ready to try a knee lock. "Keep the knee bent! Do not let him straighten you out!!" Brik shouted.

Darrin sat forward and pulled his legs back. Mahan jumped, landing his leg over Darrin's head. He slapped tight a head scissors. He tried to modify it to a triangle choke. Darrin held his legs straight so he couldn't. Mahan's legs were strong. Darrin moaned as the pressure cranked on his skull. The thick muscle around his head was like a hot vice. He was rolled onto his side and had no idea where he was.

Alex's face hovered in view. Darrin nearly screamed. *How did he get in here?* Mahan didn't react. Darrin wondered how much crazy shit Alex could do as a ghost. "Dude, he's got great legs. I know you're busy, but how does that feel?" Darrin felt the hot vice of muscle crushing his skull and smelled the warm sweat from Mahan. His crotch stirred. Alex was *not* helping.

The fists again. Mahan gut punched him hard. Darrin tightened up to withstand the pounding. Again, like a bomb in his stomach. He gagged trying to catch his breath. Darrin was proud of how his six-pack was developing, but he knew he couldn't take much more of this. Bam! That one really hurt. Darrin tried to pry the scissors off his head. Mahan cranked the pressure on.

BAM! That shot to the gut made him nauseated. He was swamped in noise and pain.

"Knee shot! Right!" Darrin obeyed with nothing left. He lifted his knee and connected with Mahan's face. The pressure on his skull slacked. He hit him again. Mahan shifted to try to block the head strikes in this tight grapple. "Heel!" He straightened his leg for a heel strike and connected with something. Mahan broke contact and backed off.

Darrin stood and turned madly to find Mahan. The ref grabbed Mahan and pushed him to the wall. He focused on Mahan and he was having his eye attended by the ringside physician. The crowd was roaring. First blood! Darrin looked around the octagon. Alex was nowhere to be seen. He looked into the crowd and saw him next to Johnson. Alex smiled and waved. Johnson had this look of horror on his face, clearly not ready for the spectacle of Darrin and his fight. He ate more popcorn and looked into the bag in disgust.

"Look at Mahan. Do not look into that crowd!! Who are you looking for? Stay here!" Brik yelled. He looked at Brik. Man, that guy was handsome. He stripped out of his sweatshirt somewhere along the way and just wore a black muscle shirt. He pointed harshly "Mahan!"

Darrin spun and fixed his eyes on Mahan. He was going to win this. He wanted to go home with Brik. The break did him good; he had his wind and resolve back. The referee signaled them to fight and again Mahan drove right into a takedown shot. Darrin timed a knee lift into Mahan's face. The takedown fizzled and Mahan was scrambling.

They met chest to chest. From the clench around Mahan's chest, Darrin cranked tight a good squeeze and lifted him in the air. They spun and landed with Darrin on top. Darrin's world erupted in pain as he collided face first with Mahan's mouth. He tasted blood and knew his eye was bleeding now. He held Mahan in place with his bearhugging clench and cranked as much pressure as he could muster. "UUUugh!" Mahan cried out in pain.

Darrin broke the bearhug and straddled his tight midsection. Darrin rained punches down on Mahan's face and head. Holding his arms over his face, Mahan weathered the thundering blows. "He's done! He's done! Knock him out!" Brik roared. Arching back on his head, Mahan executed a bridge bearing Darrin's weight on just on his feet and his head. Mahan strained his neck muscles tight in the effort. Darrin's legs slipped around his midsection and clamped a tight figure-four body scissors. The crowd howled in disbelief as the sweat and blood on their bodies helped Mahan slip and turn toward the mat escaping the knockout.

With his legs still surrounding Mahan's midsection, Darrin cranked pressure on Mahan until he was screaming with the exertion. He slid his arm around Mahan's throat and cranked tight a rear choke. The punishing triangle scissors on his waist made Mahan's breathing shallow and the choke threatened to black him out entirely. "Ok! Hang on! Ride him! Stay focused, you like this too much!" *Oh sure, why not shout to everyone – HEY DON'T FAG OUT ON THIS GUY!* Darrin was mortified.

All that changed when Mahan threw his head back into Darrin's face. He saw stars and his nose gushed. Somehow Mahan slipped and turned in his slacking grasp and faced Darrin. He rolled left exposing Darrin's gut to that right hook again. One! Two! Three! Four! Darrin was sure he could throw up now. Mahan was fighting furiously but was still clamped in the scissors hold.

Darrin turned him on his back and cranked the scissors tighter. Mahan whimpered and his face shook and his eyes clenched shut as he tightened his ripped abs to keep the tide of crushing pressure from blacking him out. The crowd roared. No one at this level of training had the power to crush a well trained opponent like this. Darrin looked into the face of this younger man trying to withstand the constricting pressure and remembered what killed Alex. "Think he looks pale enough?" Alex whispered in Darrin's ear. "He could get paler."

"Shut up," Darrin said out loud. Mahan opened his eyes and look into Darrin's. *Not you!* Darrin thought. Mahan wasted no more time. He lashed out at Darrin trying to get him to break the crushing body hold. He reached down and clasped Darrin's ankle. Slowly he pressed Darrin's legs to pry this hold off his. Darrin took this lowered guard to drive four punches to his head.

The body crushing hold broke and both men scrambled apart and tried to reestablish position. Darrin focused through the blood on his face and heard the blast of a loud air-raid type siren. Still trying to get his grip back on Mahan, Darrin fought on. The referees had to pull them apart. Mahan was the first off the mat walking to his corner. The round was over and the crowd roared, They were on their feet stomping and yelling. Brik's smile beamed like the sun.

"Darrin, great fighting! Man, you are an animal! He's younger than you and you have to put him away. Don't try to wear him down, he'll just out wind you!" Brik went on. Darrin found his mind drifting to the curvature of Brik's muscular body, the darkness and texture of his five o'clock shadow, and the dreamy light shimmering around him. Someone wiped the blood off his face and packed his nose with gauze and Brik went on drilling instruction and encouragement into Darrin. He even heard some of it. He drank as much water as they would let him.

Darrin closed his eyes, resting and getting his wind. Suddenly, warm lips pressed into his and the hottest kiss he ever had warmed his whole body. Darrin closed his eyes and drifted with the kiss. He felt warm and strong. He opened his eyes and looked into the face of Alex. "Go get 'im," he said smiling rakishly.

Reeling in shock Darrin blinked and scrambled for balance. "Whoa! Whoa! Sit still man!" Brik shouted. Darrin cleared his head and there Brik was, like he was before. "How many fingers you see?"

"Four," Darrin said. He held up two, "Two," Darrin said.

"What's going on with you? Who's in the crowd?" Brik asked. Darrin didn't answer immediately. "Him? The guy you need to fight? He's here?"

"I don't know why I try hiding anything from you," Darrin said hanging his head.

"Because you're stupid," Brik said with a smile. "Show me where he is and we'll have him removed."

Darrin smiled, "North section, guy in the suit eating popcorn..."

Brik looked into Darrin's eyes. "You're lying," Brik said. "Don't ever lie to me! We'll get to this later. Get your mind back in the fight!" and he went back into his drill. Darrin wanted this fight badly and listened closely this time. He went back into the octagon on his toes.

Mahan was toweled off, but Darrin could see his legs were shaking with exhaustion. *He's mine.* Darrin knew. The Bell sounded and Mahan looked like he was going to dive first again, but he arrested the shot, hesitant of what happened last time.

Darrin caught Mahan chest to chest and tried to turn him. Driving with all his strength, Mahan drilled Darrin into the cage wall. They rebounded and hit the floor. Darrin landed on his back.

Like a bad movie in slow motion, Mahan straddled Darrin in a mount and started hammering him with fists. He was sure he was going home alone tonight. Blocking as best as he could, Darrin knew this would end it if he didn't turn this around. "He'll win," Alex said, right next to Darrin's face. "Hit him." He thought of Alex and the golden warmth of his body. There was definitely a surge of power. He could take this.

He didn't actually feel the fists strike him any more. After about the eighth punch he grabbed Mahan's left wrist in a grip of steel and pulled it sideways to the mat. With Mahan face drawn closer, Darrin cocked his right elbow, and connected with Mahan's temple. Mahan collapsed in a slump. Quietly, lying on Darrin's chest, Mahan moaned. "Owwww, fuck."

The referee pulled Mahan off of Darrin and handlers ushered him to his gate. There was blood running down his chest where Mahan's brow opened up. Darrin rose with the referee holding his right hand in the air. "The winner by knockout at one minute and six seconds in the second round; Darrin Kraft!" The crowd roared in approval. The crush of sound in the arena was like a drug. Darrin had never felt so alive. He looked at his chest and saw the blood. He had no idea if it was his or Mahan's.

Brik came rushing into the ring and hugged Darrin in a titanic embrace. Darrin couldn't control his cock for another second.. Wrapped in his big trainer's arms, crushed in a ton of muscle, he knew he loved this. His cock ached it was so hard. Held in the air in that muscular vice Darrin humped into Brik twice, just enough to get a warm rush. "You are such a lucky shit!" Brik shouted over the crowd. "That was a nice move. I never taught you that one. You learn it watching me spar?"

"It just felt right!" Darrin said. Brik nodded and pushed Darrin to the gate. They rushed out of the octagon and down the aisle toward the lockers. Alex stood on the front seat in the aisle howling and beating the crowd into frenzy. He pointed at his chest and mouthed the words "I'm next." Worry leaked into his celebration just a bit at that point.

If Darrin had looked to the left, he'd see Johnson barfing into a trashcan after finding the used cat litter at the bottom of the popcorn bag. Instead Darrin just saw Alex warmly smiling and fade into a ghostly nothing.

"Ghosts are such a pain in the ass," Darrin said, unaware he was speaking aloud.

"You bet they are," Brik said, nodding slowly and looking a bit worried about those hits Darrin took to the head. Just at the door, a kid and a camcorder stopped them. Darrin did an interview for the gym's video series. He knew why these interviews always sounded so bad. His head was spinning and he was hungry and nauseated at the same time. They gave him some sugary sports drink. He felt it course through his veins.

He remembered getting into Brik's car. He remembered eating a light dinner, a salad and some great soup. He remembered the feeling of his trainer wrapping around him in bed, the warmth of his breath, the smell of his sweat, the thump of his heart through the plate of pectoral muscle and the feel of his ripped waist.

He remembered waking to someone sucking his dick and felt his trainer's body straddling his legs. He remembered screaming as he came and feeling bulletproof as he rolled in carnal ecstasy with this muscular hunk.

Flashes and visions of Brik chewing on his nipple, laying between his muscular thighs, his cock aching from the intensity of his erection were there. He remembered almost ejaculating while humping his cock into the big man's eight-pack.

He remembered lying on his stomach and feeling Brik cover him with his muscular bulk. He remembered feeling Brik's cock slowly enter him. He remembered feeling the furry forearm of his trainer surround him and knew this was the most secure comfort he had ever known. He remembered hearing Brik howl and collapse smothering him in his sweaty furry bulk.

And in between all of this he dreamt of Alex; of wrestling him and of his funeral; of his sunny smile and of his ashen grey appearance after his insides were crushed in Darrin's bodyscissors. His eyes burned with tears as he woke. The morning light brought the certain understanding of what it was like to be haunted. Brik held him as he sobbed. He assured Darrin that he's seen it all and this was typical emotion after such a hard fight, especially the first fight.

Darrin knew that every victory, every triumph, every simmering joy with his muscular trainer, would be tainted by the memories of the friend he killed. Maybe it would be different when he put things to rest and finally sent Alex back to where ever it is ghosts go. He knew he had to beat Alex and make him say he surrendered.

He rushed home to dress for the office. His whole body hurt everywhere. He showered and shaved and saw the bruises on his face that couldn't be hidden. He didn't care either. He walked into the living room and as if on cue, Alex lounged in the living room.

He sipped on Darrin's Sapphire Gin bottle, "Tonight," he whispered and winked. Darrin tried not to cry as Alex disappeared. He was so tired. He grabbed the car keys. Just before he opened the door the doorbell rang. Darrin opened it and found a flaming paper bag on his porch. He just looked at it and shook his head. "Thanks Alex. I can always count on you for a flaming bag of dog shit." In the house he heard Alex's howling gales of laughter.

CHAPTER FIVE

Johnson had this smirk all over his face. He was wearing his red "power tie" to the meeting. It was obnoxious red with comic book yellow ducks. It really didn't matter what he was dressed in, Darrin would think he looked like an ass.

Darrin had a black eye and bruising on his face. It was nothing compared to how his body felt. He took six Advil. Little, Yellow, Useless. Cold clouds, rolling over Lake Erie, covering the Pittsburgh area that forgot winter was over, made everything hurt.

He slowly sat at the meeting table as people milled into the board room. Jennifer walked into the room like a diva in a music video. She wore a grey pinstripe suit, long red nails, and spike black heels. The black sunglasses and the two improbably huge diamond earrings completed the set. Kauffman wandered in carrying his coffee and no papers. Trent sat at his seat looking like hell, sipping coffee with too much whisky in it. The smell alone would get most people fired. "Okay, people! Let's get started." The door closed.

"Darrin, before we get to the Simmons accounts, tell me why you're a pro wrestler in your off time? Company policy states that all public appearances by management employees must be cleared. Isn't this a clear violation of company policy?" Kauffman looked at the folders on his desk, shuffling things around. This was done without eye contact. Just standard operations; Darrin Kraft smiles, apologizes, grovels, and we move on to the next.

Darrin made it longer and more inconvenient than that. "I'm not a professional wrestler."

"Oh, really?" He said, looking at Darrin finally. "Why then, were you featured as one of the newest hot performers at Manson's Arena last night?"

"I'm a no-holds-barred fighter," Darrin said. "It helps me get out aggression." He hoped this was enough threat to make Kauffman know he should leave it alone.

"Oh," Kaufmann said. "What's the difference?"

"A professional wrestler works a theatrical performance from a preset script. A fighter enters the octagon to face a real opponent, beat him, and go home." Darrin said flatly.

"People pay admission to see this event. It sounds like a public appearance to me. Quit this stuff now. Ok, the Simmons account has been looking..."

"No," Darrin said.

Kaufmann tried to look tough about this. He took off his reading glasses and turned, "What did you say?"

"I said no," Darrin said. "I put in nearly two decades with this company and have made you tons of money. You could've had the decency to have this conversation in private like you did with Trent and his drinking and Johnson and his child abuse conviction." Trent choked on his coffee cocktail, spewing half its contents across the table. "So my answer to you is no."

Jennifer looked up from her notes slowly, while Kaufmann turned red. "Clean out your desk. You're fired! No one talks to me like that!"

Jennifer didn't skip a beat. "Here's the new schedule. I have Johnson taking most of Mr. Kraft's responsibilities and Shirley Kelso making a step up to Finance Operations. She looked at Darrin and smiled thinly.

Darrin got up slowly and gathered his notes. With a deep breath, he walked out of the boardroom. He felt nothing. He was going to go home to the house he could no longer afford and drink whatever hit his hand first and go to bed and rest. He found himself in the break room. He walked to the far end to the water cooler. He looked out the picture window there at the manicured lawn and rolling hillside. The walnut trees were coming into leaf. Darrin knelt before the water cooler with his mouth on the spout; he took a good long drink.

Johnson came into the room laughing. "Oh man, you have a great way of ending a meeting. Kaufman went to his office foaming. He called the whole meeting off and left," he said pouring a cup of coffee. He stopped and looked at Darrin on the floor. "Nice fight last night. I'm surprised you walked away from that. That kid was a monster..."

Darrin stood and closed the distance between him and Johnson with a determined stride. Johnson fumbled with his coffee, sure Darrin was going to hit him. Darrin grabbed Johnson by the throat, "That *kid* is a bigger man than you'll ever be, asshole. He was a tough opponent and I beat the shit out of him. You should be personally concerned about this."

"If you hit me, I'll sue you for everything you have!" Johnson howled, trying to cower against the wall.

"Well, that's very encouraging, you know. I don't really have much without this job. Did you arrange your promotion with this?" He slapped Johnson in the face with a crack. Johnson howled like he was being tortured. "Jennifer had the new schedule ready, you *fuck!*" He slapped Johnson again.

"They paid me to follow you!" Johnson sniveled. "I just wanted a raise out of this!"

Darrin had heard enough. He lifted his knee into Johnson's gut driving the wind out of him. Shrieking in pain and fear, Johnson clung to the wall. Darrin looked at him in the eye. He was about the same height as Darrin, He even looked trim and fit. He was just another coward. Darrin decided that he should never resemble Johnson again. He dropped him on the floor in a sniveling heap.

Johnson took two heaving breaths. "I'll sue you and that little blond boyfriend of yours. He put cat shit in my popcorn."

Darrin just stared at him. "Boyfriend?"

"That Alex kid," he said getting up off the floor. "I'll kick his ass if I ever see him again."

Darrin just nodded slowly, "I'll let him know." Darrin slowly walked out of the break room, happy to leave that scum behind.

Trent walked to his car. He begged Kaufman for the rest of the day off. He wasn't feeling well. Without argument Kaufman just stared out the window and said, "Go."

Darrin walked past him on his way to the car. "Later, Trent," he said. "Get help." Trent nodded. Just as Trent was about to say something, they were distracted by a crash of broken glass. They looked at the building in time to see Johnson fly out the second story window of the break room and roll down the hill. He rolled across the nice lawn and came to rest against one of the walnut trees. He stood, staggered, and fell flat on his face. Darrin could hear Alex laughing. "Did you see that! Haw! He fell on his face!" He howled another chorus of rakish laughter.

"Better get some rest, Trent," Darrin said. "Tomorrow's going to be real busy. Congratulations on the promotion." Trent just stared, slack jawed. He reached into his car as Darrin walked away and grabbed a bottle of Ole Granddad. He looked at it and looked at Johnson flat on the lawn. He shook his head and dropped the bottle in the back seat without drinking a drop. Darrin's Fiero drove away, coughing smoke, to the approaching sound of ambulance sirens.

The sun set taking the gray day to darkness slowly. Darrin stood in his living room stripped to his waist, still wearing his office pants. He did his push-ups and stretched for about 20 minutes.

"You ready?" Alex's voice came from behind him.

"You didn't have to hospitalize Johnson," Darrin said. "It won't change him a bit."

"Someone had to. He sucks," Alex said with his usual rakish smile. He walked into Darrin's kitchen and opened the fridge. Unwrapping a packaged of sliced ham, he turned to Darrin. He took a bite out of the ham nodding his head. "So," he said with his mouth full. "You gonna kick my ass now?"

"If I have to," Darrin said quietly. He squared himself slowly for any sudden attack. His chest rose and fell showing the new muscle he put on in a month's time. Alex walked up to him and slowly ran his hand through the hair on Darrin's chest. Darrin was still amazed at how warm Alex seemed.

"Nice muscle dude," he said quietly. "You even have abs now."
Warm hands ran over Darrin's shoulders. "Wow, muscle here too.
You've been working hard. You know, I wish I had chest hair.
Think I'll ever get any?" Alex said with a smile.

"No, you're dead," Darrin said.

Alex nodded and tossed the half-eaten ham over his shoulder
and said, "Okay, let's go!" He lunged at Darrin, slapping him in
the chest with both hands. Darrin tumbled backward, landing on
his feet in front of the eastern bay window. "Hey, that Brik dude
taught you some cool stuff." He slowly walked around the living
room. He dove to take Darrin down. Darrin sprawled his legs
backward going to a front facelock. They were wrestling and not
fighting. He didn't know what rules Alex was going to use in this
fight. He presumed none.

Right on cue, he felt Alex grab his nipple and pinch hard.
"Aaaaahh, shit!" Darrin yelled pulling his hand off his nipple.

"I always wanted to do that," Alex said. He chuckled as his legs
squeezed down on Darrin's leg, cutting the circulation off in
Darrin's leg. Throwing his right elbow back toward Alex's head,
Darrin turned onto his back. "On your back, now you're pinned,
dude," Alex said.

Darrin was fighting for control of hands not caring about being
"pinned." He was going for submission. "Right, submission,"
Alex said as though he heard Darrin's thought. He slapped his
hand over Darrin's right pec sinking in a claw hold. It felt like
he could drive right through his ribcage behind his pec. "Oh
it's a claw hold! Can he get loose!" Alex shouted imitating a pro
wrestling ring announcer. "Naw, he's a pussy and he's going to
submit..."

"But does he want to get loose, that's the question, Mean Gene," pretending to be a gruff color announcer. Alex loosened the clamp on Darrin's leg and slowly began to grind his thigh into Darrin's crotch. "Just like the Old Days, ain't it?" Darrin felt Alex's body heat and still found he was unable to resist his beautiful friend. His cock was hard leaving him writhing in pain and pleasure. He planted his hand on the back of the claw hold, trying to pry the fingers out of his chest muscle.

"I'm so glad you like this part," Alex said. "I do too." He laid his face next to Darrin's ear and began to slowly chew on his neck. Darrin could feel the ripped muscular body of his long gone friend. He was flooded with memories of his aching want for Alex. Slowly he released the claw hold on his chest and put his other arm around Darrin's neck.

"You cheat, you bastard," Darrin said putting his arms around Alex. Alex's hot lips met his as they rolled on the carpet together. Darrin could feel Alex's hot cock drive into his abs. He moaned in pleasure.

"I sure do," Alex whispered into his ear. "So you gonna fuck me tonight?" He asked hotly in his ear. "Or is this just reserved for your trainer?" He grabbed Darrin's throbbing cock. Darrin's head arched back in deep pleasure. He had always wanted Alex. Resistance to him was impossible.

He rolled Alex over and covered him in a deep kiss. He reached his hand under his Eagles T-shirt and felt Alex's silky skin. His cock was rock hard and he knew he could fuck Alex all night if he would let him. Looking into Alex's eyes, he saw a golden light get brighter as Alex's hands explored his body in return.

"I love you Alex," Darrin finally said.

The fire in Alex's eyes grew brighter and brighter. Like he could no longer contain the inside joke everyone else knew, Alex burst into laughter. His hand fired into Darrin's throat and locked in tightly. "You are so stupid! I really thought this would be hard, but here you are giving me everything I need to end this!" He rolled Darrin over onto his back. Darrin gagged at the powerful constriction closing in over his throat. I was going to give you the chance to beat me. I even thought that was the easier way. But I found you giving me power more and more over these past weeks. I can end this if I end you!"

Darrin hammered on Alex's hands and forearms. His mind sparkling with oxygen deprivation. *He might succeed...* Darrin thought for a moment. He pulled at Alex's pinkie finger and pried his right hand loose. Alex quickly freed his finger and began wailing punches into Darrin's face, his left hand still tightly wrapped around Darrin's throat.

Alex back his ass over Darrin's shrinking cock, "Still want to fuck me? I have no idea how much power that would give me. Maybe that would be real fun. He unbuckled Darrin's pants and started to tear them from his body. Darrin choked trying to recover his breath. Alex's brought his face to Darrin's waist and began to kiss his stomach lightly while massaging Darrin's cock. He was still hard and not softening a bit, in spite of Alex's assault.

Alex looked up into Darrin's eyes and lifted a closed fist. "This will be amazing," he said. His eyes were glowing a golden color. He clenched his fist tightly as it glowed white, leaving a ghostly trail as moved. Darrin was prepared for a punch. He instinctively lifted his leg protecting his balls. Alex blocked that with his body. He opened his hand and gently cupped Darrin's balls in the glowing white light.

Darrin was instantly consumed in a desperate hunger. His body arched backward howling in ecstasy. He stripped his Eagles shirt off and straddled Darrin. "Do you want this body?"

Darrin, unable to stop himself, rolled Alex on his back. He lifted Alex's off the ground as he tore his shorts from his body. He rolled Alex on his back and threw himself on top of him. "Woah man, I guess the flowers worked," Alex smarted back. Darrin wrapped his arms around Alex's torso, squeezing him as tight as he could. He hips took a rhythm.

"Come on Darrin buddy, put it in me," Alex coaxed. Darrin was overwhelmed by the smell and silky warmth of his buddy's back and shoulders. It was like he was so many years ago. He felt his cock land against Alex's hole and want to thrust inside him so badly. He pressed and suddenly felt the coldness inside. *This is wrong...*

"Do me, buddy, this is it! Do me!" Alex pleaded. *This is wrong. Oh please stop me...someone help me please. I don't want this...* His cock hurt it was so hard. His guts were cramping he wanted to cum into him so badly. Alex pushed his ass back into Darrin. He felt his cock slipping into the unfeeling coldness. *NO! NO!*

There was a knock at the door shattering the moment. Darrin pulled himself to his knees and sat back. He was alone on the living room carpet. He heard that he was screaming with every exhale of breath. The door burst open and Brik strided in brazenly. He knelt in front of Darrin and tried to hold him.

"DON'T TOUCH ME!!" Darrin screamed.

Brik's huge hand lightly smacked Darrin in the face. "Hey killer, It's me..."

"I didn't kill him! Stop it! It's not my fault!" rolling tears fell from his face as he collapsed into his trainer's arms. He cried convulsively.

"I know," Brik whispered.

Alex moaned, "Just kill me now, please..."

"Don't talk crazy, ok?" Brik whispered.

"You know," Darrin said breathlessly. "Today, talking crazy is real easy."

The tea tasted great. The rest of the world was draped in shit colored gray. But the tea was marvelous. Oh, and so was the deep brown color of Brik's eyes. He was so patient with all this weirdness. He knew it was impossible to repay him. He would just have to try.

"So I came in when he was raping you?" Brik asked gently.

"I couldn't stop. But I know better now. He gets stronger with my desires for him. I hate to think what would've happened if I fucked him. He would've been strong enough to kill me."

The front door opened and closed. "Honey, I'm home!" Alex chimed. Brik was on his feet immediately, standing between the front foyer and the kitchen. Alex was dressed as usual, but seemed dim in color, unsmiling. Alex has two bags of groceries in his arms. Milk, eggs, veggies, real household stuff. Brik tried to block his entry and Alex walked through him. "Nice try, meatbag," Alex said passing through. He set the groceries on the counter. Brik found himself touching his body and shaking.

"That's creepy you know," he said.

"So kill me," Alex retorted.

Darrin let out a deep sigh. "What are you doing here?"

"I brought some stuff to eat," he said, avoiding eye contact. "The cashier was cute and he just let me have all this stuff for free." The room remained silent. "OK, you're welcome."

"What do you want?"

"Oh, ok. We're finishing this. Tomorrow at the gym, in the ring, 10 PM," Alex said.

"And if I don't show?" Darrin asked.

"Then it'll happen where ever you are," Alex said evenly. "You will beat me, or I will just kill you. I can do it now. I learned a lot tonight."

"And so did I," Darrin said standing. "Get out of my house!"

Alex laughed, "You know, that was almost convincing."

Darrin walked just a bit closer to Brik and held his hand. Brik stood stone faced and squeezed Darrin's hand back. Darrin turned to Alex, hissed, "I said get out." Alex vanished on the spot. They stood, hand in hand, together in the kitchen.

"I might not be able to defeat him," Darrin said. "But I know we can."

"I'll clear the gym," Brik said.

VOICEMAIL SIX

Brik posted the special hours the first thing in the morning. By mid-morning, the regulars wanted to know why. By noon he had agreed to relent and tell them one of his students was having a very special fight, and let them presume it was for a big promoter. And they complained when they found out that was Darrin and how does he rate after three months of training and yadayadayadayada?

By the time eight o'clock rolled around and Darrin walked in, Brik had shed his pleasant metro sexual man image and became the don't-fuck-with-me warrior. When he announced it was closing time, it wasn't a request. "Closing now! Get out!"

The regulars that had fought with him or been taught by him knew that tone meant that you can dress outside and moving now is good. The new guy in the back was finishing slowly. "Darrin, could you be the nice guy and get that jerk moving? I'm done being nice today." The Old Darrin would've sulked that his coach was yelling at him. This new Darrin knew the pressure of the coming moment.

The new guy was hammering away at the heavy bag like it had personally offended him. His form was scattered but his intensity was sharply focused. He hadn't done this in a while, or maybe never. He was pasty white and hadn't seen the sun in years. Sweat poured off him in rivulets. "Hey dude," Darrin started. The guy stopped and looked Darrin in the eye. "Hey Darin, good to see you..." it was Trent, the alcoholic from work.

Darrin stopped and stared. He realized his mouth was open. "Uh...Trent. Nice power. Get with Brik on Monday and focus up your form."

"You bet," he said toweling off.

"We're closing early so you need to go. Brik is very focused and wants everyone out," Darrin said.

"Yeah, I heard earlier,." Trent quickly moved. "You going up against that kid that kicked Johnson's ass?"

"Um... yeah, hey, let's talk more about this after the weekend, I mean if we see each other." Darrin fumbled.

"Oh, I'll be around. Let me know all about it," He walked in close and gave Darrin a hug that lingered a beat longer than necessary.

"Good luck," he said. "I know you'll win." He broke into a quick run for the door. Darrin heard the door latch shut with a snap. Brik walked up behind him.

He grabbed Darrin by the face, using deep his brown eyes to drill in the point, he let out a deep sigh. "I'm not losing you tonight."

"Ok," Darrin said weakly. "How are you?"

"It's strange, ever since last night, I've been full of energy and ready to wrestle 20 foot pythons." He said with his first smile since Darrin arrived.

"Uh... can I watch?" Darrin asked.

"It's the second fight after yours," he said. "Hang out for it. It's a killer match-up." He rubbed the growing muscles in Darrin's neck. His hands were strong and warm. Darrin was amazed at how that power and strength got him horny. Just as he began to lean into his hands Brik's coach face arrived on cue.

"Ok, Tommy and I are setting up the space and he goes home to Linda knowing nothing. You go to the locker room and wait for me to call you out at 10. I'll be in to check on you. Do your warm ups, Tommy will come in with pads and gloves for that. Hit him as hard as you want. He's young and should heal." He smirked for that one. "And, most importantly, picture yourself winning and saying good-bye. Don't even flirt with failure."

"Yes sir!" Darrin said.

"I'm keeping this formal to limit the number of surprises he's going to pull. You keep yourself in focus, got it?"

"Yes sir!" With that he walked into the back room. Darrin walked into the locker room and turned on the lights. He looked around cautiously, wondering why the lights were off. Water dripped from one of the faucets back in the shower room. He put his things in his regular locker. He stripped and looked in the mirror at his new body, forged mostly by terror. He flexed a double bicep pose and loved the big bulge that was there. Maybe it was always there, leftover from College, but just neglected. "I'm not losing this. Never!" He was serious.

He sat on the bench, bent over his shoes, fixing them tightly in place. Maybe it was something in the air, but he knew Alex was there. He sat upright and looked around. Nothing.

He bent over to tie his left shoe and he felt a light kiss on the back of his neck. He had to sit upright quickly to accommodate the instant erection. A warm muscular arm slowly circled around him from behind, stroking his chest. Hot breath fell on his ear, his eyes unfocused in ecstasy. A strong hand stroked the light fur in the center of his chest. Darrin pulled down his sweat pants, his cock jutting above his jockstrap. A warm hand quickly cupped his balls and gently massaged them.

"Squeeze me Darrin," said Alex said breathlessly in his ear. "I love it when you squeeze me... to death."

Darrin quickly leapt to his feet and turned. He was alone in the lockers hearing just his screaming breath. His cock was throbbing. Just then Tommy walked in. He was a tall black guy in his twenties, his body iron-hardened by years of training. He stood holding his pads and gloves and looked at Darrin and his protruding cock. "Let's get ready to warm up, ok?" he said. Darrin frantically assembled himself. "Hey hey, don't worry man," Tommy said. "Every dude has his prefight rituals. I just found that if you save that shot for later, you tend to fight better."

"Thanks," Darrin said. His heart was rattling. *No more sexual traps.* He promised himself. "Good point. Let's get started."

Ten o'clock was near and Darrin waited on the mat standing next to Brik. He wore a pair of lycra square-cut briefs and nothing else. The room was quiet and still, strangely absent of the music that usually thundered through the room. The climbing rope gently swayed under the air conditioning fans. The punch clock in the office beeped and Brik said. "It's ten." He walked over to Darrin and looked into his eyes. "Have you decided how this is going to end?" His blue eyes were penetrating and serious.

"Yes. I'm winning and continuing my training with you," he said evenly.

"Keep that in place," he said.

They turned and there was Alex standing in a broad stance. He actually glowed with a golden aura. His body exuded an attractive warmth. "Thank you for coming," he said. "I'm sorry about last night. I don't know what came over me. We'll do this as long as we need to"

Brik turned to Darrin, "Ok, stud. Don't believe that crap about being nice. He set the rules for tonight. Don't be taken in." Darrin put in his mouth piece and pounded his gloves together.

The gameplan was still a bit unclear. Defeat Alex, but how? What defeats him? As Alex closed and began to circle, he could feel the arua of warmth he was generating. *He was never this warm. He must be very strong right now.* Alex dove for a single leg takedown. snaring Darrin's right leg. Darrin sprawled pushing Ales away.

It was Alex's shoulders that were the first thing Darrin's hands touched. The muscle there felt strong and warm. Darrin's cock stirred. As though Alex could feel it, he began to giggle. "Man, that stiffie gets you into some amazing trouble." Still holding Alex's leg, he moved his hand up into his crotch as his other arm clenched Darrin's neck and shoulder.

Darrin reacted to protect his crotch. He knew Alex was trying to make this encounter sexual, the heart of Darrin's previous wishes. He swung at Alex's face driving him back. Alex backed off and rushed in with a quick flurry of punches. They were really wild and over swung leaving openings for Darrin. He took one. POW! Connecting with Alex's jawline, he spun and backed off.

A normal man would've been stunned by such a solid punch. He drove in to tie up with Darrin unfazed. Darrin was leaning in just a bit and Alex exploited his balance and pulled Darrin's head forward, lifting his knee to Darrin's face.

Darrin reeled feeling himself get thrown and mounted. Alex straddled his torso and rained punches into his face. He suddenly slid his knees back toward Darrin's feet planting a vertical elbow into Darrin's gut. He stood up and walked around the ring, triumphantly holding his hands overhead. Darrin rolled in pain, trying to get the spasms in his solar plexus to stop. He felt blood trickling down his face.

Brik urged Darrin to get up. "Listen to your love and get up...here I come." Alex said with a sinister tone. He stripped off his Eagles T-shirt and threw it aside and ran toward Darrin. He bared to the world that beautiful torso and those gleaming muscles.

Darrin tried to kick his support, but Alex dodged his kick. He dropped all of his weight on Darrin with his knee; a direct shot in the gut again; Darrin's air expelled from him in one rush.

Giving Darrin no time, he drove his fist into Darrin's abs. Trying to knock the driving fist away, Darrin swung. Alex took the moment to drop his crotch over Darrin's face, wrapping his legs around his neck. All Darrin could feel was the smothering heat those muscular legs and smell the musk of his crotch. "You suck Darrin," Alex smirked. "And now you'll prove it." As he cranked his legs closed around Darrin's head, he drilled Darrin in the guts three times.

Pulling Darrin's head forward, Alex forced Darrin's face right over his hard cock. Darrin could feel that beautiful cock pushing through his shorts. He wanted Alex so badly his vision blurred. *This is an attack. He wants me aroused.* Darrin knew and fought harder to get out of this hold.

Alex groped Darrin's crotch with a gloved hand. "Man what a great cock you have. For me?" he said, releasing the neck hold. He fell on Darrin's crotch chewing his hard cock through the black lycra shorts. Darrin nearly shot, screaming with overstimulation.

He remembered Tommy's hint and held back his load with everything he had.

Brik watched, keeping his distance. If this was going to come out in Darrin's favor, he had to do it. But he was surely not going to sit and watch him get killed either. "Darrin, knees!! Kick now!!"

Darrin heard Brik shout and drove his knee up. Just reacting and not watching, he kicked. He felt Alex's teeth crunch into his knee. He drove again but this time harder. Alex fell back holding his face. "You fucker," he moaned plaintively.

Darrin rolled and scrambled to his feet. Alex slowly rose holding his face. "That hurt man. I beginning to think you don't like me any more." He looked at Darrin's crotch. "But I see you still want me. How touching."

"If you want to think of horny thoughts, Darrin, you think of me!" Brik shouted. Darrin wiped the blood away from his nose. It dropped on the mats freely.

Alex dove for another takedown. Darrin met his lunge with another knee aimed at his face. He missed. Alex easily caught his leg dumping Darrin toward the mat. Darrin connected Alex's head with three solid punches. Alex drove his fist into Darrin's crotch.

Darrin screamed in agony and rolled. He felt his pubic bone just throbbing. He cried, blood mixing with tears of pain. Darrin instinctively rolled to get away from another ball shot. Alex slipped around behind Darrin snaking his arms around Darrin's throat. He locked on a rear naked choke. Darrin's vision began to fade, his body a riot of pain. "Don't you quit! Elbow strike then turn!"

Darrin drove his elbow into Alex's ribs repeatedly. Alex just tightened his choke. "I get to go home. What a rush!" Alex crowed. Brik ran over to interfere and felt something land on him from above. It was the climbing rope from the ceiling. He looked up expecting to see who was there. The rope suddenly coiled itself around Brik's limbs. It grew thicker and moved just like a snake.

"We can't have you interfering, Brik," Alex said. "So this is as close as I could come to that 20 foot python you requested." Coil after coil of rope as thick as his arm wrapped around Brik's body. His legs were immobilized and he found himself unable to reach Darrin.

Darrin pulled forward as hard as he could, kicking his legs up to nail Alex with another kick. Alex just surrounded Darrin's waist with his legs to hold him tightly in place. They locked in tight and began to squeeze. Darrin pulled on the choking arm hard and bought a breath. He grabbed Alex's pinkie and pulled hard. The choke came open and he tried to turn in Alex's scissor hold. The squeezing pressure cut into his waist stopping his struggles. Darrin grabbed the top foot and lifted. The hold broke, allowing Darrin to breathe again.

Brik could get no closer to Darrin and Alex, He groaned as the rope coiled around his torso, under his armpits, pulling tighter as each second went on. A coil encircled his muscular neck and he struggled with the coils to keep his breath. The rope was slowly enfolding him in a constricting embrace.

Darrin turned as saw the predicament Brik was in. He turned pummeling Alex with a flurry of punches. His eyes were closed and couldn't see where Alex went. He took two deep breaths and looked to see Alex scrambling backward, holding his face, trying to recover.

He scrambled over to Brik and pulled at the constricting coils. Brik's face was red with exertion. The muscular cords in his neck stood out betraying how much crushing pressure he was under. He looked up at Darrin and gasped, "Finish him..." Blood trickled from the corner of his mouth. Darrin saw his new love slowly being killed and began to panic. He looked into Brik's blue eyes and wondered how he would live without him. But then he stopped *aren't his eyes supposed to be brown?*

Darrin scrambled away from Brik and glared at Alex. As though he couldn't contain an inside joke, Alex burst into howling laughter. Brik and the rope vanished. "You little shit, where's Brik?" Alex just howled, rolling on the mat. "What did you do to him?"

Alex grew serious. "I said I learned a lot last night," he smirked. "I have your beefy boyfriend now."

"NO!" Darrin shouted refusing to accept this. "WHY? Just leave him alone! It's between us!"

"Yeah, but you guys double teamed me last night," Alex said with a sneer. "I'm coming to like the idea of destroying you. Maybe both of you." Alex leapt to his feet and rushed Darrin. Battered, pained, and lost, Darrin put up frantic resistance.

He punched Alex in the head several times and then turned to body shots. Alex was overwhelmed by Darrin's power. Darrin's mind returned with a spark *I have to decide how this ends.* "GO AWAY NOW!" He shouted. "I don't want you any more."

Alex found himself floundering. Darrin straddled his waist, raining punches and elbow strikes. He grabbed Alex's head and rolled him forward. Just like he did long ago, he clamped his legs around Alex's torso and locked them tightly. Alex took a deep breath and held onto Darrin's leg, offering little resistance. He gasped, clearly in pain. A resigned look crossed his face.

"Good bye Alex," he said. He flexed his legs and poured on as much pressure as he could. Alex groaned in agony, the last strains of his voice strangled away. His golden aura receded, turning ashen grey. Darrin hammered punched into his face and chest. Any normal fighter would've been crying for quits.

"Give?" Darrin asked. Alex's eyes closed and his head shook.

"You make this sound like it's easy..." Alex gasped. Darrin added more pressure, pulling from somewhere. Alex's head kicked back and he groaned in agony. "Give up!" Darrin shouted at Alex.

What if he can't be beaten this way? He swam floundering for a solution and it occurred to him *Bring the wish to an end.* Darrin crushed Alex as hard as he could, remembering the moment he wished for his dead friend. He pulled Alex's head to his face and kissed Alex deeply on the mouth. Coming up for air, he noticed the relieved look on Alex's face. "I'm sorry you died. I never blamed you," he whispered.

Alex looked relieved and a small tear leaked from his cheek. "Take everything back now," he whispered and kissed Darrin again. All the energy form all the years of wanting came back to Darrin as Alex drifted into transparency. There was slowly less and less for Darrin to hold. In the end, he laid there on the mat holding himself.

He stood hearing the eerie silence that had descended on the gym. He looked up to see the rope still in place and heard the air conditioning shut off. It was truly quiet then.

"Brik?" Darren called out. He slowly walked to the front office calling his name. A gauzy blue light filled the room and leaked from under the door. A man in a fighting gi stood in front of Brik, his arm extended to a single pointed finger, touching Brik in the chest. Brik stood frozen with a look of shock on his face.

"I see you're finished," the man said, not moving his hand. "Well done." It was Jim Wise. Darrin remembered him from his picture. He turned to face Darrin and revealed the horrifying damage left from the wreck. "Do not be disturbed by my appearance and never deny a warrior his scars. Stand behind him. I'm about to release him and he might falter."

"Is it over?" He asked Larry. "I mean the fight with Alex."

"Is it?" he asked back in return.

"Yeah, I am sure now," he said, completely realizing that his desire to see Alex again would need to be arrested for the rest of his life.

"He may reincarnate like everyone else," Larry said in response to the quiet question. "But you know he shouldn't rush into that. Catch now..." He released Brik from the blue aura and he quickly blacked out, collapsing into Darrin's arms. "His interference would've just made things worse. Good bye." He said. Darrin looked up and saw no one else in the room. Brik's brown eyes fluttered open.

Darrin and Brik were awakened by the sound of hammering in the front yard. They had managed to get home and just collapse. The gym was still set as a fight arena. They were twined in each other's arms, Darrin had one sock on, out of gas during his strip. Brik was ready to rise and looked outside. "It's some guy hammering a for sale sign in your yard."

Darrin groaned. "It's always something..."

"No it isn't," Brik said lowering himself on top of Darrin. Their lips met and he ground his crotch into Darrin's. "Now that," he said coming up for air, "Is always something."

"Ok, you win this time," Darrin managed a smile. He put on his sweats and walked outside. Trent was wiping his hands off and looked up at Darrin. "Great morning, isn't it? Did you win?"

"Um... yeah I did." He paused and stared at the sign in his yard. "Uh, Trent? Have I been foreclosed? My payments are current for now."

"Um, no. I took some liberties this week. Since I'm replacing you at work and they always expect me to fuck up, and you left your signature stamp in your desk, I had Kauffman buy your house."

He handed Darrin a check. Brik, dressed (just barely) in workout shorts walked behind Darrin in time to catch him as he staggered back in shock. His beautiful musculature shown in the sun through the forest of fur on his chest. Trent could see how truly huge Brik was. "That's a lot of zeros." Brik mentioned.

Trent stammered, "Um, yeah. I really suck at paperwork so I didn't notice we were buying it for 2 mil." He suppressed a smile, the first genuine one Darrin ever saw Trent have.

"That's four times the value of the house!" Darrin said.

"Call it back pay," Trent said putting his hammer in the trunk of his freshly cleaned car. "If they don't like it, they can fire me." Trent shuffled some papers around. He handed papers for the sale to Darrin as well as some tax information. "Oh here, this as well."

Darrin read it and stared at Trent. "You're evicting me?"

"Yeah. It's not your house. You have 30 days. Go buy something else..." he said looking at Brik. "Something bigger, with a big bed, maybe." Brik flexed his pecs and Trent laughed. Trent looked over Brik's shoulder and said, "Your cat just caught something."

"I don't have a cat," Darrin said.

"Oh, well you better get him out of the house. He just walked inside." Trent got in his car and rolled down the window. "Oh guys. I'll see you at the gym in the afternoon. I need to work on my form." Brik nodded.

Darrin walked inside staring at the check. It looked real enough. He looked at the couch in the living room and saw a burly male orange tabby chewing on a package of hot dogs. Darrin approached slowly. Brik came behind him and reached for the cat., slowly. The cat lunged for Brik's forearm hugging his wrist. He brought up his hind legs and wrapped them around his forearm. Brik lifted the cat and gave it a shake. "He's on there. And never put a claw on me."

Darrin put his face closer to the cats. "Alex?" he asked. The cat purred loudly. Darrin opened the package of hot dogs and the cat dropped to the floor mewling loudly. The package ripped open with a pop. Hot dogs scattered all over the carpet. The cat grabbed one and slipped under the couch.

Brik and Darrin looked at each other. "We're moving."

Take of fertile earth as much
As either hand may rightly clutch
In taking of it breathe
Prayer for all that lie beneath
Lay that earth upon thy heart
And thy sickness shall depart
"An Ancient Charm" by Kipling

ABOUT THE AUTHOR

Living in New Mexico, raised in Pennsylvania, D Douglas Erickson started writing muscle and wrestling stories in 1997. He's catered to a group of men that love men and muscle and the rough-and-tumble lusts they have. For ten years his works have been praised as hot and sexual with heroic muscular men, evil muscular villains that get off wrapping the hero in a body crushing bear hug or bodyscissors.

Since leaving Pennsylvania, the sheer numbers of men that have had their true sexuality discovered in front of the television watching pro wrestling came to love Erickson's work.

Growing up in Pennsylvania, where nearly every boy wrestles as a past time, he quickly fell in love with The Wrestler; the solid man of muscle and discipline that played by the rules. His works examine that man and his ability to endure hardships. In that worship, he wrote many stories featuring the men of his dreams. He always thought his admiration was somehow alien and not shared by others. With the advent of the internet, he found he was not alone.

www.ingramcontent.com/pod-product-compliance
Lightning Source LLC
Chambersburg PA
CBHW071227260626
47162CB00004B/1445